JORDYN MERYL

THE SPACE BETWEEN

jmdragonfly, LLC.

Also by JORDYN MERYL

Novellas

When Dreams Change

The Trouble With Angels

Home Before Dark

Coming in 2013

Novels

Becca's Dance

Katie's Wind

To my grandson Bryce

and

Bob Dylan

Thank you Beta Readers

Danielle

Tina

Jennette

Elle

Rachel

The Space Between
by Jordyn Meryl

Published by jm dragonfly, L.L.C.
Des Moines, IA

ISBN-13:978-1481047814
ISBN-10:1481047817

Copyright © November 2012
By Jordyn Meryl
Published by jm dragonfly LLC

This book is a work of fiction. Names, places, characters, and incidents are either the product of the author's imagination, or if real, used fictitiously. Any resemblance to actual events, locales or persons living or dead is entirely coincidental.

All Rights Reserved. Except for use in any review, the reproduction or utilization of this book in whole or in part in any form, electronic, mechanical or other means, now known or hereafter invented, including, photocopying and recording, or in any information storage or retrieval system, is forbidden without the written permission of the author.

Thank you for respecting the hard work of this author.

First Printing: November 2012
Printed in the United States of America
Cover Design-EJR Digital Art-www.ejrdigitalart.com.

PROLOGUE

"Where are you, bitch?"

His words sounded just before the door flew open with an echoing bang. The man walking in as ominous as the black clothes he wore. Close to six feet tall, with a forbidding presence of darkness and extremely handsome, he brought with him an air of fear laced with danger. A raging anger preceded his words spoken with a sharp, piercing accent on his displeasure. Throwing the tabloid he gripped in his hand at the woman standing at the counter cutting vegetables. Her wide eyes betrayed her panic. Keeping her poise, she did not speak to the man's insults.

Her right hand gripped the large kitchen knife as her left hand reached for her cell phone. Hitting "1" on her speed dial, she sent the call as she backed away from the man.

"So, I read in the rag paper, you accepted a modeling assignment in Paris. Of course after hearing it from a friend' who couldn't wait to rub it in." The very tone of his voice made her jerk with alarm.

On the move, to get far away from him. "...it just happened this afternoon. I am preparing a sumptuous meal for us to celebrate." Waving the knife towards the chopped food.

Her first instinct to come home, pack and escape now looked like the better choice.

Jordyn Meryl

Her back hit the wall as he reduced the distance between them. He lunged forward and with one swift move, backhanded her. The knife and the cell phone flew from her hands as she slid down the wall to the soft white carpet.

The explosion in her head put flashes of light in front of her eyes. The cell phone was within in her reach. The knife was not. Snaking her hand out she tucked the cell phone next to her, careful not to hang up.

The woman stood up slowly, the sting of his abuse still radiated on her skin. "But it's my job. It's what I do." Swaying wobbly, she leaned against the wall trying to clear her head of the pain. "It's a good-paying gig." Her hand with the phone hung at her side she turned towards the wall.

His sinister laugh told her that was the wrong thing to say. "You have a job. Pleasing me. You don't need money. I meet your needs."

His advancement towards her again made her step away. "Okay, I'll call." She turned towards the bedroom, walking on unsteady legs.

In the room, her bags stood packed, ready to go. With the caller still on the phone, she picked up her bag and purse. She needed to escape. To get away from this madness.

Wheeling her suitcase behind her, she shook her head again to clear it then went out to face him.

From behind the counter, his eyes flashed an intense fury as he watched her come out of the bedroom with her luggage.

"I see you are not taking me seriously. Do I need to make my point clearer?"

Stopping short, she raised her head and squared her shoulders. "No, you made yourself perfectly clear. I am leaving, you and this toxic relationship. Good bye."

With her courage tucked under her arm, she gripped her bags, still holding the cell phone gently in her hand.

A terrifying level enragement radiated from him. Grabbing the knife, he met her at the end of the counter. His hand tightly grabbed her upper arm stopping her in her tracks. She faced her demon.

"What are you going to do, beat me into submission? Fine, but I will heal and someday at some choice time I will escape you."

The blade of the knife and his vermin words echoed through her body at the same time. "No, you stupid bitch. You will never leave me alive."

Searing pain grabbed her as it sent her to the floor. Grabbing her stomach, feeling the warmth of the blood pouring from her, she watched as it flowed through her fingers. The overpowering stench of death insulted her nose. She could feel her life ebb out of her. An anger so strong it made her shudder, rose like bile up through her soul.

<u>I am going to die. You stupid bastard. I will make you pay for this.</u>

The darkness came as a welcome cover. Her hand closed over her cell disconnecting the person on the other end.

Jordyn Meryl

CHAPTER ONE

Live long, love deep, walk strong...
***

"God, Mitch you are fucking pathetic. It was right there."

The sun tanned, well-built young man put his hands in front of the other man's face, fingers spread as if holding a ball. "You suck, dude."

The one called Mitch laughed a deep, warm hearted laugh. He acted as if he had no idea why he missed the ball. No, he knew, the beautiful woman crossing the beach and his line of vision. Beautiful? More stunning. Distracting him from his game of beach volleyball.

Where'd she go?

Of the two men, Mitch knew he could pull off being the better looking. His best friend, Stanley, who hated the name, so they called him Snake, the jokester of the bunch. Not a bad looking guy, but loud, abrasive, obnoxious and a jock with no interest in ever being tied to a woman. Mitch, on the other hand, loved women. Loved being with them, their smell, the feel of their skin, the sound of their voice. Especially their taste, he loved their taste.

And he had just been smitten by the most gorgeous looking female he ever saw. Her movement over the uneven sand of the beach could be a graceful dance. The sun seemed to surround her with a glow like a spot light.

Okay getting a little carried away here. No woman is that great looking.

Then his gaze found her, sitting under a palm tree, the shade creating shadows on her face. Slender, her elegant shoulders taut. Long black hair fell down her back almost to her waist. Straight and full, the light breeze moving it only slightly. The long white skirt she wore fell gracefully to the ground. Her legs crossed, it showed slender, long limbs, just enough to be tempting. Correction, she was that great looking. Her beauty took his breath away and also his concentration.

The ball hit him in the head. He let it bounce off, not feeling anything other than a rising desire to go over to her.

"Damn it, Mitch, where's your head?" Snake picked up the ball and slammed it against Mitch's butt. "Wake the hell up."

If this is a dream, I don't want to wake up.

In a trancelike state, Mitch moved towards the woman.

"Dude, where are you going?" Snake's voice shouted behind him.

Waving all concerns away. "Later." His body kept moving. The closer he got, the more his stomach tightened. He never before felt reluctant to approach a woman, this one possessed something different.

When close enough to share the shade with her, she looked up at him, titled her head and smiled slightly.

Not knowing where to put his hands, he leaned one against the back of her chair, bringing him nearer. As beautiful close-up as from a distance, she captured his curiosity.

"Hi."

Great starting line, idiot.

He held his breath waiting for her response. If she told him to get lost, he would understand.

"Hello. . .?" Her voice sounded like a sweet melody.

". . .Mitch." He stuttered.

Cool. Not

He wanted to know her name, but his brain couldn't find his mouth to tell it what to say. "And you. . . .?" He waved an open hand.

When she smiled it took his breath away. He hoped he could see her smile a lot.

"Katrina." It rolled off her tongue with a slight accent from. . .he didn't care. She existed here now.

The words started coming from his mouth, Mitch couldn't stop them. "I'm over there playing beach volleyball with my friends. . ." He pointed over to the guys and noticed they were standing in a line staring at him, but he didn't care. ". . .and I saw you walk by. . ." He would rather look at her. Absorbed in her exquisiteness, he looked down. ". . .like 'The Girl From. . .someplace, it's a song, and I had to come over. . ."

". . . Ipanema.'" She injected.

Her voice stopped his on slot of words. "What?"

Faint laughter and her smile put him weak in the knees. "Ipanema. The song is 'The Girl From Ipanema' and thanks for the compliment." Her violet eyes sparkled like a brilliant cut gem.

Hook, line and sinker she reeled him in. His knees collapsed. Not even searching for a chair, he went down cross-legged on the cool sand. Now she towered above him. Her out stretched legs were just inches from his face. His eyes traveled up her legs to her waist and over her breast to the beautiful face. She watched him. Embarrassed, he could not take his eyes off of her.

"Um. . ." He cleared his throat. ". . .you live around or on vacation?"

Jordyn Meryl

He felt her intense look go deep into his soul, making him a blubbering idiot, when usually he pulled off being Mr. Charm. She seemed to relish his discomfort.

"I'm thinking of moving here." His heart jumped against his chest he almost didn't hear her next question. "Do you live here, Mitch?"

"Kind of. We're filming on the beach." He pointed his thumb behind him. "Staying here for six months."

"At the hotel?"

"Yes, at the hotel. . .Are you staying here?"

Please, please, please.

"For now I am staying with a friend at a beach house just a way down." His heart sank. She has a boyfriend, or husband. Her expression made him think she could read his thoughts. "A girl friend."

Well, okay this sounded better.

Gathering his courage. "Would you like to have dinner tonight?"

Her infectious smile made him think 'yes'. "I would love to, but not tonight." Somehow he felt she left a promise.

"Another night?"

"Yes, most certainly another night." As she rose and towered over him, to keep his eyes on her face, he craned his neck back. The sun moved casting an angelic glow around her. Without a word, she drifted away from him. He watched until she became lost in the crowd.

The hand slapping his back brought him out of his trance. "Hey Mitch, what is going on with you?"

Mitch stretched his body as he came up from his setting position. "Did you see her?"

"Who?" Snake looked around and then back at his friend.

Mitch stood confused.

How could they not see her? The most beautiful...

"The girl?" Using terms, he knew Snake would understand. "The hot babe I was talking to. How could you miss her?"

"Didn't see her. All I saw was you carrying on a conversation. Your body blocked the person."

Not possible the guys would have missed such a fox.

He searched the people, looking in all directions. But she vanished like a vapor. Looking at Snake, he knew they weren't pulling his leg.

"So what's this vision's name?" Snake inquired.

"Katrina."

"Like the hurricane? Katrina what?"

"Just Katrina. And why did you call her a vision?"

"Because, dude. If you are the only one seeing her, it's a vision. Let's get a beer."

The guys left him standing alone next to the chair.

Well, he saw her. Not a vision. The realest woman he ever met.

He knew he would have to see her again.

***

Katrina stood on the side of a sand dune, watched the guys of the beach trickle up to the bar. Mitch by far the best looking. When he spoke to her, his electric blue eyes flashed with mischief. Stumbling over his words, she got the impression he usually could be a lot smoother in his approach. His sun-bleached hair cut short, but if it grew long she imagined it curly. Dressed only in swim trunks, Mitch looked tight and fit. Almost hairless, his chest bronze and Greek god-like. Mitch stood probably close to six feet tall. Any girl would swoon at his feet. As she cocked her head, she saw several were.

Mitch approaching her took her back. Not that men didn't approach her, but his spirit seemed different. Never before could she sense such a pure heart. There was a spiritual connection like a magnet.

A large wave crashed over the sea barrier she stood next to. The thin mist filtered over her skin, touching it in a calm, peaceful way.

Trust him.

Her soul echoed the energy Mitch oozed. A strong, but innocent force of gentleness and compassion. She figured she would have no one to trust. An undertaking of solitude and isolation. Her battle. Her demon. Her ultimate right to correct an outrageous wrong.

His body movement and grace were why she stayed to watch him. A group of friends and strangers greeted him. His responses were always warm and friendly. Famous in a sea of fans, she knew his type. Cool, confident and ego driven. But he was not of the same mold. His aura was a swirl of greens and yellows with a bright white crust cruising through the vortex of colors.

Since "the accident" Katrina developed a spiritual insight used to guide her along her course. Having made the decision to extract the revenge she deserved, she avoided people who wish to connect with her. Usually she moved unseen through crowds. Why Mitch saw her and pursued her was not what she expected. She came to the hotel to familiarize her soul with the locality, the feel of the place. Many factors needed to come into alliance before she could expect Tomas to arrive.

The sun set over the Pacific Ocean. The bright, glowing reds and orange were to Katrina's back, but she could feel their colors across her skin. Soon darkness would envelope the beach, and the moon would cast its eerie shadow over the dunes. She needed to search for the core of Mitch as he slept.

***

After midnight, Katrina stood under the window of Mitch's suite. Raising her arms towards the wall of vines, she closed her eyes and entered his dreams. With a smile, sensing his desire and pleasure, she bowed her head and allowed the images to encircle and tantalize him.

Her will explored his soul. Finding a genuine and untainted life-force, she became aware of an affection building for him. If to be a part of her design, he would instinctively bring the gifts of his spirit to the surface.

Time would tell.

Jordyn Meryl

CHAPTER TWO

When early morning finally dawned, Mitch had been awake for two hours. Having already drunk a pot of room service coffee, he sat in a chair on the balcony outside his room, his feet propped up on the rail. Since he faced the west towards the ocean, he only saw the sun coming up in the movement of the shadows along the sandy beach.

His night had been full of sexual dreams of a beautiful woman.

Through a mist, he saw her among the voids. Her back to him, the long, dark hair fell to her waist. A soft light outlined her body, sending out spikes of color. He moved in slow motion. Anxious to get to her, she seemed far away.

Slowly, she turned to watch him approach. Her smile made her whole face sparkled. A long, silky, thin fabric covered her, but the light allowed him to see her body. Letting his gaze travel down, her full breasts pushed against the low V cut of the material. Curves in the right place, his eyes followed them to her thighs. Long and smooth his first thought, he wanted them wrapped around his waist. His manhood grew the closer he came to her.

A connection of souls made his desire for her seem almost mystical. Not the normal, hard coursing desire, but a sweet want to connect with her over whelmed the usual strong sexual craving. Reaching her, he went to his knees as a powerful link to beauty felt forbidden to him. His hands reached out to touch her. Putting both hands on her waist, he buried his face in the cloth, sucking in the smell of jasmine and musk. Her hands touched his shoulders. As he lifted up, she lowered her hands to his unclad chest, her touch cold. He shivered.

His eyes searched her face, her amethyst eyes flashed with bright silver sparks. With his hands still on her waist, he pulled her into him. Her smile hid a trace of naughtiness. His lips wanted to taste her. Feeling her body form into his, he...

Half awake, he reached out for her, searching the bed, he patted and probed. Finding nothing, he sat up and ran his hand through his hair. Bewildered and disappointed, he realized he was alone in the bed, his body covered in sweat.

The dark of the night mocked him. The clock said four am. Sleep would never come, so after a frugal try, he shucked the covers back and left the bed. Unsure of what happened, he stood in the middle of the room looking for a hint. He had dreamed of women before. But never so realistic, so orgasmic. He needed something normal to do. So he walked over to the phone, hit the room-service button, ordered coffee. His body felt heavy, still moist from the dream.

A long lukewarm shower.

Welcoming the stinging water as it hit his skin. It confirmed he was awake, his dream was just a dream. Leaning his back against the wet wall, his mind could not clear itself from the mental picture of Katrina. Yes, he knew it was her. She affected him different than any other woman, like a cross of tangible and imaginary.

Stepping out of the bathroom, dressed in jean and a v-neck tee, just as the knock on the door and "room service" echoed in the room. He opened the door, paid the waiter and poured the hot liquid, taking slow sips as he allowed the caffeine to rejuvenate his body.

The sky lightened as he slid the glass doors back and walked out into the brisk sea air. Running his tongue over his lips, he tasted the salt.

The Space Between

The breeze moved across his face. Try as he may his mind stayed obsessed with images of Katrina. His need to find her burnt like a hot coal in his stomach.

Putting on his logical mind, he pushed his passion aside and concentrated on what she actually said yesterday. 'Staying on the beach with a friend a ways down.' Figuring down should be south, he looked each way and saw several beach houses both large and small. If he just kind of 'wandered' down the beach maybe he would get lucky and find her. Or he could sit all day and wait for her to show up. No, a man of action, he went to comb the beach until he found her.

The cool, smooth, morning sand imprinted his footsteps as he ambled down the beach, acting like out for a splash in the ocean, carrying his shoes in his hand, his pants legs rolled up. He scanned the houses lining the beach. Having no idea which one could be the right one, he felt on an idealistic mission. Still, there was hope.

"Looking for me?" The sweet female voice startled him.

When he turned, his fantasy from yesterday stood before him looking more radiant than he remembered. Like him, her jeans were rolled, her shoes in her hand. Her denim shirt hugged the curves of her body, around her neck a stone of milky white to silver. Her dark eyes told him of a depth to her, he was ready to discover.

But first. . .he reached out and touched her hand. Real. Flesh and warmth just like everyone else. Snake must have been messing with him.

She titled her head still waiting for his answer.

"Yes, I'm looking for you."

"Very ingenious of you to find me so quickly. Are you a private eye on the side?" Her smile lit up the lovely, flawless face.

Mitch felt relieved to find her. She genuinely existed. "No, just on a mission to find the most beautiful woman who brightened my day yesterday. Thought maybe she would grace me with her presence over a cup of coffee?" He couldn't stop the smile overtaking his face.

Linking her arm in his, she steered him towards one of the massive houses on the beach. "I have a pot on. I walk while I waited for it to brew."

Hugging his arm, they walked together towards a light taupe house sitting back from the others. Climbing up the deck, he took in the large windows and contemporary design. The house reflected the girl, but. . .

"You said you were staying with a friend? This house suits you."

Reaching the top, she released him. "It's a friend's. Amber. She has exquisite taste."

Sliding the glass door, she motioned for him to sit down on the deck. "I'll be right back."

Climbing up on the stool at the table, he watched the waves ebb calmly from the beach, leaving the smooth, untouched sand behind. Lost in his thoughts, her brushing his arm as she sat a cup down in front of him, brought him back to the present and why he wanted to be here. He never believed in love at first sight or soul mates or any of that. If you were to ask him right now, he was falling for Katrina, fast and hard. His gaze settled on her face as she took the stool across from him.

"You are so pretty, are you a model?" It wasn't a line. She looked familiar as if he had seen her somewhere before.

Sipping her coffee, her smile implied he guessed right. "Yes, I was, am. Taking some time off."

"Why?"

Her eyes took on a faraway look. "It's a long, unpleasant story. Not something I want to think about right now, okay?"

"Sure. So what's a nice girl like you doing in a place like this?" An old line, an old joke, but serious. He wanted to know anything she would be willing to share.

A wry smile turned her lips. "I am just enjoying the peace and calm of the beach before starting a new...assignment."

"Modeling?" His heart sank fearing it would take her to some far-off place.

Running her finger around the rim of the cup, she lowered her eyes. A slight pause, but it spoke volumes to him.

"If I am intruding, I'm sorry. You are just so fascinating to me. I keep asking questions." He stumbled over his words. Last thing he wanted was to drive her away.

With her eyes still down, she shook her head. "No, questions are quite all right..." Raising her violet eyes to lock on his. "It's the answers I find hard to voice."

"You don't have to answer them." He leaned back in his chair.

Her face softened. "It's just I have some unfinished business I need to take care of. A messy, distasteful, loose end must be resolved."

"So you'll be here awhile?" He wanted to know.

Biting her lower lip, she chuckled. "For a while. I am waiting for someone to arrive. It might take a while for them to get here."

Another man? Don't ask fool.

"An old flame?" He did it anyway.

"Sort of, but not what you think."

How do you know what I think?

He grinned awkwardly and cleared his throat. "I try not to think."

Lifting a firmly arched brow, she gave him one, long searching look. When she spoke, her voice seemed cold and steady as stone. "It's a payback for an unjust act. But not to worry. It will be over quickly."

Mitch reached out for her hand. She didn't move it away. Rubbing his thumb along her index finger. "I won't worry. Do I have to wait until it's over to see you again?"

Her hand took hold of his, squeezed it lightly. "No. What I do need not depend on what I must finish. Come see me anytime."

The large steel clock in the next room struck eight times.

Mitch jumped up. "Shit. I need to go to the set. Later?"

Katrina stayed seated. "Yes, later. Bye Mitch."

He wanted to kiss her, but felt awkward. Instead, he just turned, leaped down the deck stairs and jogged towards the hotel.

***

Mitch left the beach house with her eyes on him. Without losing sight of him, she took the cups with her as she entered the house. Sitting them down, she walked over to the large windows, placing her hand on the glass.

Oh, Mitch. I wish we had met at another time. It could have been very different.

"Are you going to tell him about Tomas?" Her friend Amber waited until Mitch left to come out. Amber's real name was Margaret Gross, but her auburn, naturally curly hair made the name Amber fit. Like Katrina, her exquisiteness shone as flawless. They were both the same startling beauties, but so different in coloring.

Just the name of Tomas felt like the knife plunging into Katrina again. Her hatred for him peaked at immeasurable.

"I can't. It will put him in danger." Sorrow washed over her. She could not explore a long-lasting relationship with Mitch.

Amber started to reach out to touch Katrina's shoulder. "You came here to set a trap for Tomas. Mitch will get in the way." She let her hand drop.

"I know, but if only. . ." Katrina could not even finish the thought let alone the sentence.

If only Mitch came first instead of Tomas, maybe she would have had a chance at happiness and a true love.

Amber's words were filled with the compassion she felt for her friend. "I know, the 'if only' will haunt you forever. I am so sorry."

Katrina turned and looked at her dear friend. "It's my fault. I wanted the glamour, the money, the prestige of being with a powerful man. I paid for it. . .am still paying. But the time will come when I will make him pay. And pay dearly. He will know how it feels to be in confinement for his sins."

Turning back to watch the figure of Mitch grow smaller on the beach, her heart ached.

Such a foolish mistake. To have the chance to escape from Tomas and to have waited too long.

A mistake would forever be her burden.

***

The large shape of Snake loomed before Mitch as he crossed the sand and up to where the cast for the day stood around waiting for instructions.

"Hey, Bro." Mitch's hand smacked his friends back.

The shock and glare of Snake's eyes were followed by his angry words. "Where the hell have you been? I beat on your door forever this morning."

Jordyn Meryl

Mitch nonchalantly strolled by him, a smirk on his lips. "Out. Walking on the beach." Extending his arm out towards the beach, he hit one of the girls who played an extra. "Oh, sorry, didn't see you."

Her fierce look surprised him. "You never have."

He grabbed her arm. "Excuse me?"

Letting his hold remain, she frowned at him. "This is the fifth episode I've been on."

Releasing his grip, he dropped his hand to his side. "I'm sorry. I just sometimes don't notice people."

"Yeah. Sure." With those final words, she walked away.

Mitch turned to Snake, whose arms were outstretched in a 'whatever' gesture. "What the hell?"

The director shouted into a large bull horn. "Now that Mr. Mallord has chosen to join us, let's get to work people."

Mitch felt stunned. First, the girl, now Cap, it started out as such a pleasant day. The crowd moved to their places.

Snake hit him on the back. "Forget it. But. . ." He made Mitch stop with him. ". . .where were you?"

"I told you. On the beach." Mitch faced his friend his face emotionless.

Snake formed a smirky smile. "Did you find her?"

Mitch, close to losing his cool. "What makes you think I'm searching for a 'her'?"

"Must have been the vision from yesterday." Snake patted Mitch's face in a quick, patronizing way.

Mitch's ire came up. "She's not a vision, she's real."

Lifting an eyebrow. "You find her?"

Mitch looked away, then back. "Yes I did."

Snake gave him a sharp look. "Did you touch her?"

Mitch countered attacked. "Yes and she is flesh just like the rest of us."

A wicked, natural smile curved Snake's lips. "If you say so, buddy."

Mitch grabbed Snake's arm. "What's your problem?"

"Nothing, dude. If she is real, bring her to the party tonight." Snake heaved a sigh, slipped his hands into his pockets.

Mitch let go of Snake. "I will. You'll see."

The Cap's booming voice could shake the ground. "People are we ready yet?"

Jordyn Meryl

CHAPTER THREE

As soon as he could get a break from filming, Mitch ran down the beach to the house he visited just this morning. On the deck sat a young woman, with an oversized straw hat, reading a book. Her ginger colored hair wispy around her pretty face.

Approaching the stairs to the deck with caution, he shouted up. "Is this where Katrina is staying?"

The girl lowered her book and looked at him over the cover. "Yes, Mitch this is the place." The way she answered him with such familiarity somewhat took him back.

"Have we met?" He started up the stairs one at a time.

"Not formally, I'm Amber. . ."

". . .Delaney." He finished for her. He recognized her from the magazines. Known as a super model. Big name in the industry. Big endorsements. "Do you model with Katrina?"

Sadness flashed across her face. Her eyes took a faraway look as if he disappeared. Then she seemed to focus back on him. He didn't understand her distance stare, but he had seen it in Katrina's eyes. Amber gave him a slight grin. "I did, when she modeled."

He watched her deep emerald eyes to see if he could read anything, he felt she wasn't telling him something. "She said she's on a break. Why?" The question came out before he could stop it.

Amber laid the book in her lap. "Yes, she's on a break. But she will tell you when the time is right. So what brings you by, Mitch?"

Jordyn Meryl

"Oh, well the cast is throwing a party tonight at the hotel. A winding up this episode type thing. I wanted her to come."

A small smile turned up her lips. "I'll tell her."

"Where is she?" He didn't mean to be intrusive, just kind of wanted to see her.

"Out, she went out."

Mitch accepted getting information out of these two women not always easy. He started to turn away, a though struck, he turned back. "Say, if you would like to come. . .?"

Amber nodded. "Thank you. We'll see." With her elusive answer, she dismissed him.

He finished his exit from the stairs. At the bottom, he turned and waved at her. "See you tonight."

Waving back, she said nothing. He saw a look of reserve. Shrugging his shoulders, he left the way he came.

Katrina appeared at Amber's side.

Amber looked up at her friend. "So are we going?"

"Yes, we are going. What harm can it do?"

***

When the cast put on a party, it could only be called a massive event. Loud music echoed up and across the dunes. Large fire torches lit up the sky, no mistaking where to gather. Lots of rich, sumptuous food and drinks a plenty. A bight colorful affair, which made the beach people swell with merriment as they migrated.

Katrina stood on the edge of the crowd, watching all the happy folks enjoying each other.

How long since I enjoyed the person I came with? High school?

After graduating, she worked and worked, leaving little time to socialize. Men were always attracted to her, but she went only for the powerful ones. Enter Tomas with his dark, good looks and his command of individuals.

Her prince.

But his obsession became a prison surrounding and smothering her. Just feeling the freedom of walking into a party and not seeing him presented itself as a gift.

Mitch over by the bar, leaning against it, ignoring everyone around him. She watched his light indigo eyes searched the crowd. The knowledge he looked for her made her feel wanted for her, not as the arm candy of some egotistical man.

Amber stood at her side. "Are you ready?"

Katrina shook her head. "No, you go on. I need to savor this moment. It may never come again once Tomas believes I'm still alive. Then I will need to be as far away from Mitch as I can."

Amber nodded her understanding. Moving through the crowd, she grabbed a glass from a waiter's tray. Standing by a tree, she waited. Katrina lingered with apprehension for the moment when Mitch spotted her.

His head slowly turned as he searched the faces in the crowd. Then he noticed her. His body straightened, he moved with the easy of a cat through the crowd of people to her. His eyes fixed on her face. When he came close, he let his gaze travel down her body. The black halter dress she chose hugged her figure like liquid satin.

His pleasure at having her here increased the smile on his face as he raised his head to look at her. "You came."

She took his hands, held them out in front of them. "I did."

"You look fabulous. God, you are beautiful." He leaned in and gently kissed her cheek.

Jordyn Meryl

Her senses savored the feel of his lips, the scent of sand and sea water on his skin. Allowing herself a second to experience it all in case it became the last time.

Facing her, he smiled a crooked grin. "Amber?"

Katrina nodded her head to her right. Mitch's eyes followed the gesture and saw Amber by the tree. He grinned and nodded. Amber raised her glass as a salute to the two of them.

His attention went back to Katrina. "Can I get you a drink?"

"Wine."

Mitch's head turned towards one of the several waiters carrying a tray of filled crystal flutes.

"Champagne?" He asked back over his shoulder.

Katrina released his hands. "Perfect."

As the waiter passed, Mitch grabbed two glasses. Handing one to her, he clinked her glass. "To a delightful night."

Her eyes watched him over the rim of her glass. Infatuated, she could tell. She always produced an effect on boys since junior high. Usually she was flattered but uninterested. But with Mitch she felt different. It was more than refreshing. It was an urge in her for it to be real. Even so, until she dealt with the past, nothing was real.

Mitch acted giddy. He took her hand and pulled her gently towards a group of young macho studs. "I want you to meet someone."

Her spirit flooded her with heat. She had known this would happen. Glancing back over her shoulder, Amber pushed off from the tree and followed them. Katrina's hand in Mitch's felt warm, comfortable, following his lead to the bar.

One of the young men downed shots followed by beer chasers. Just the kind of jocks she avoided most of her life. He turned when they approached. Getting his full attention, his eyes obvious in their once over of her. His low whistle raked on her nerves. All his actions appalled her in every way. Lifting her head up, her bare slender shoulders back, her breasts pressing against the fabric of her dress, she took a deep breath.

Even his voice raked on her last nerve. "Ah. . .the vision. You are real. I didn't believe ole' Mitch here, but. . ." His leer oblivious and unmistakably rude. ". . .you are most obviously real, baby."

The word 'baby' spoke enough to make her want to cut him to shreds with biting, unforgiving words. Tired of men thinking wearing their sexual proneness on their shelves proved a way to impress a woman.

Her anger fired up from the pit of her stomach to her chest. Her breast heaved with fury. However, then she felt Mitch's warm hand squeeze hers.

No, my annoyance is not at this stupid person in front of me. My bitterness is deep and dark, and I must not display it here.

Glancing over at Amber, she returned to the phony, superficial person she conditioned herself to be when needed.

"Thank you. . .?"

Wiping his hands on his pants, he stuck out his hand. "Snake."

Since one hand held a drink, she released Mitch's hand and took Snake's. "Snake? Really?"

Mitch laughed his delightful laugh. "It's a nickname. His given name is Stanley. Stanley Greene."

Katrina did not want to crack a smile. What she wanted to say tittered on the tip of her tongue. Cruel biting words that could bust a man's balls. But she relaxed and said simply. "Indeed." As her grip tightened on his hand, she felt her fire of anger burn his palm.

The look crossing Snake's face seemed to be one of bewilderment. Katrina let her hold remain as she watched him squirm.

Jordyn Meryl

Enough of this nonsense. He is a harmless stranger. Not the one you are angry at.

When she finally released her grip, he shook his hand as if to get the feeling back.

She turned her attention to Mitch. "Can we go somewhere and sit?"

"Sure." He took her hand back in his. "Excuse us guys. The lady and I would like to be alone for a while."

Katrina turned to Amber. "Are you okay for a while? You can come with us…"

Amber looked pass Katrina and Mitch, settled her gaze on Snake and his gang. "No, I'm good. Just come find me before you leave, or if you decide to stay the night with beach bum gorgeous, let me know." Her quick smile gave Katrina a welcome relief. Hugging Amber lightly, she turned back to Mitch.

As she followed Mitch to a table, she looked back and saw Snake' eyes watching her. His forehead wrinkled, his eyes narrowed. Doubting feelings betrayed him. Maybe this wasn't a best idea to come to be with Mitch.

Mitch lived in a world of people and friends and wanting to know what a person did. She could not be in his world. Her world consisted of dark, shadowy secrets, she needed only one thing.

***

The party lasted long past midnight. As the moon broke through the night clouds, Katrina, Mitch and Amber walked down the beach on soft, cool sand. The waves broke quietly on the sloping shore. The horizon became nonexistent. No line between the water and the sky, the air a little chilly, a little breezy.

Mitch and Katrina spent the evening together laughing, talking and dancing. He still could feel her soft curves and long lines of her body when he held her close. She enveloped him in a drift of exotic perfume.

Nevertheless, she told him nothing more about herself. When he saw an opportunity to ask her, she seemed to perceive his unspoken question and turned his mind to something else.

Reaching the beach house, Amber went up the stairs and left Mitch and Katrina alone. Mitch pulled her into his arms. Her soft, firm body melted into his. Burying his face in her hair, he took in the smell of jasmine. Usually Mitch knew all the right words to say, but tonight he could not find any words to tell her how passionate she made him feel.

As she turned her head to him, he met her lips in a searing, hungry kiss, savoring the sweet tang of champagne. As he intensified his kiss, she moved her hips to fit into his. His hands moved down her back to the top of her waist. She pulled his shirt open, running her long finger nails over his chest, leaving a thin line of blood. The pleasure mixed with pain made his desire rise. She stopped him as he started the pull her down to the sand.

Her words came firm, but kind. "Not yet, darling. Soon but not now."

Oh, gawd.

His body became aware of being on fire. He wanted her bad. Breathlessly he asked. "Why?"

Laying her hands on his chest, she massaged his skin as her eyes held his. "I need to take care of some things, and you need to know what's in my past. In time, Luv."

"So there will be another time?" The joy inside of him jumped.

Katrina tossed her head back and laughed. "For tonight you need to go to your room. Meet me here later this morning. The light of the day will make it easier to tell you." Her words were mysterious and intriguing.

Not actually wanting to, he agreed. "I will be here at dawn."

Her smile turned out to be the sexiest he ever saw. "Dawn. Good things happen at dawn."

***

After Mitch departed, Katrina went into the house to stand behind Amber watching her worked the keyboard on the computer.

"The nearest I can get to Tomas is the south of France. He has a website searching for you, but I can't tell if he has connected you to California."

"You've sent inquiries?" The edge in Katrina's voice carried a harsh tone. Apprehensive, she wanted him to find her. It had been a painful wait for a year to extract her revenge. Just didn't want to make it easy for him. Too easy and he would get suspicious.

"Yes, but I am trying to be evasive. It's impossible to track the source. I want him to think there is still a hidden agenda. He will dig deeper. A prize too easy will bore him. It's the only way to bring him out." Amber looked up at her friend.

Katrina patted her friend's shoulder. "Keep at it. I want him here. I want him trapped and then the whole world will know what that scum of the earth did to me."

***

Cursing under his breath, Snake kept rapidly moving his fingers over his laptop. Everything he entered about the mysterious Katrina came back she died a year ago. Yet he just held her hand. It felt real all right, but there happen to be some kind of compelling force behind the grip. When it started to tighten on him, he watched her eyes. He knew she did it. And she quietly challenged him to defy her. Releasing the vise, she looked innocent and unknowing. His palm still stung from some kind of heat she inflicted.

Watching her and Mitch all night, Snake kept getting this uneasy feeling about the beautiful woman who swept into Mitch's life. Like a phantom, she existed but did she?

Pictures of her flashed across his screen. A model known for her beauty and charm, she did magazines, catalogs and runways. Until a year ago, when she started to be listed as deceased.

From a stabbing, by a boy friend.

Mitch and Snake had been best friends since grade school. He would walk on fire for him. If he was happy, Snake would be thrilled. However, an uneasy feeling made goose bumps rise on his arms. This did not thrill him.

Jordyn Meryl

CHAPTER FOUR

The young man at the computer pushed away from the desk and walked into the sunroom where his boss leisurely indulged in a mid-morning bunch. "Tomas, we have another hit on Katrina."

Tomas lowered his newspaper. "From where?"

"California again, Santa Monica. The third one, but this one is different."

Tomas' attention peaked. "How so, Peter?"

"I can trace it. The other two I couldn't." Pushing his black-rimmed glasses back up his nose, the geeky, looking assistant stood at the end of the table. Nothing less than business first, no sense being anything other than professional with his employer.

The dark eyes of Tomas held the man's gaze, a small smile played at his lips. "I see. And what did you find when you traced it." The directions were implied.

Peter knew what would be asked of him, and he did his work well. "It came from a computer owned by a Stanley Greene. He is a bit player on a TV series called "Law Out West". They film on the beach at Santa Monica."

Tomas leaned back and studied Peter. "Is Katrina on the show?"

Peter shook his head. "No, there is no evident she is doing any acting or even modeling. But this Stanley shows an interest in her and hit every site."

"And why would he a year after she supposedly died in a tragic accident?" Tomas' voice laced with sarcasm.

Jordyn Meryl

The words 'tragic accident' made Peter shiver. He knew what happened the fateful night. He helped Tomas escape the country. Together they lived a lavish lifestyle in the South of France. The USA couldn't touch him. Plus Peter happened to be his alibi. He covered for his boss, was paid handsomely for it, why he did it? Fear claimed to be his motivator. Tomas would have hunted him down until he found him, then kill him in one of those 'unfortunate accident'.

All the reports came back to Tomas stated Katrina died. But Tomas never accepted it. He personally did not see her in the casket. Even when the police woman came to France, Detective Chris Graves, to question them, he still doubted it. His suspicions they were hiding her from him consumed his every waking hour and had for a year. Peter hoped she was dead. If Tomas ever found her, he would make sure her life would be a living hell. Death would be a relief.

Tomas rose slowly. "I think it is time we took a trip, Peter. California sounds inviting. Make the arrangement. Book us at the finest hotel in Santa Monica. On the beach. I so love the beach."

"Do you think it is safe? They can arrest you if you are in the states."

Tomas swept his hand in the air. "Pashaw. They will have to find me first. We will be in and out like this." Tomas snapped his fingers.

Peter bowed. "Yes Sir. When do you want to leave?"

Tomas swept his large body around and started for the door. "As soon as possible. Charles, I need to pack. Peter, tell the pilot to prepare the plane."

***

When Katrina looked out the glass window at the early-morning sunlight creeping across the beach, she saw the familiar outline of Mitch sitting on the steps of the deck. The sound of pushing outward on the French doors made him jump up and turn around.

A sheepish grin on his face. "You said dawn."

She leaned on the door, her long, silky robe brushed her feet. "So I did. How long have you been out here?"

As he started up the stairs, she liked the way his firm body, in jeans and a white v-neck t-shirt, moved with each step. "Since about three."

"Did you go home?"

Coming up to her, he put one arm around her waist, his lips touched hers delicately, with a feel of desire. "No, no reason to. I wouldn't have slept. So I just waited here."

Yielding to her desires, she kissed him back. Wrapping her arms around his neck, she buried her face in the sweet warmth of his chest. He shifted her body back inside the house, his hands moving down her body.

Laughing she pulled away from him. Taking his hand, she led him to the kitchen where two cups of coffee waited for them. Motioning for him to sit down, she sat across from him.

His face showed his impatience. "What is it you need to tell me that I have to wait to make love to you?"

Covering the mug with her hands to feel the warmth, she watched the liquid swirl around. "I was in a highly toxic relationship."

"Are you still?"

"No, I am out of it, but. . ." Her eyes searched his face. ". . .he is still looking for me."

"So. He can't have you."

His naive outlook endeared him to her. "It isn't that simple."

Mitch grabbed her hands, his voice carrying an edge of determination. "Yes, it is."

She didn't want him involved, maybe she was wrong to bring him into this mess. "Listen. It's dangerous, real dangerous. I want you to let me deal with it and then. . ."

He finished her sentence. "...we can be together."

She wouldn't make promises she couldn't keep. "I just need to deal with this, okay?"

Mitch's eyes narrowed. "I won't let him hurt you."

The mixture of determination and caring made her essence ache. "He can't anymore. But he can hurt you. And I couldn't stand it."

Confusion clouded Mitch's face. "Why don't you just call the police?"

"I did, but they can't do anything. They tried, but he is smart and tricky."

"What can I do to help?" No ultimatum, no argument. Just his offer of support.

She wasn't used to the pure actions of a good man. Tomas always made her decisions for her.

Katrina now wanted to be done with the payback she needed to inflict on Tomas. The sooner the better. "Just let me do this my way."

His face told her of his concern, his hands squeezed hers. "Okay, you got it, but. . ."

"If I run into trouble, I'll let you know." Her fingers traced his fingers, intertwined with his.

He lifted her hand to his lips. Kissing it tenderly, he spoke with his eyes.

This man would never hurt me. He would go to the ends of the earth to protect me. But it is him I will protect. Tomas must not know about Mitch when he finally does find me.

The large grandfather clock struck six. A frown crossed her face. "Go, nothing going to happen now." She released his hand. He reached out for hers, but she pulled it back.

"I can stay." His eyes pleaded with her.

"Later. Come back later. Go sleep now." She stood up.

He rose with her. Without words, she came to him. Her lips traveled up his neck to his lips. Using her teeth, she took his bottom lip into her mouth, let her tongue move sensually. His moan matched his body movement to merge them together. Her body responded as she relaxed against him.

When she moved back, his eyes were closed. In a low voice, she told him. "Come back to me."

***

Standing at the glass looking over the ocean, Katrina felt Amber behind her.

Amber's voice cut through Katrina's thoughts. "Did you tell him?"

Closing her eyes tightly, she swallowed. "Not all. Some."

"I just checked the computer, Tomas is on the move. He is leaving France."

Katrina didn't turn around. She just looked at the sparkling waters crashing on the sand. "Where is he going?"

"California. Santa Monica."

Those were the words Katrina wanted to hear. "Good."

It was fresh air she needed as she walked out and down the deck to the beach. At the edge of the water, she stood to allow the wind to surround her like a cocoon. She could sense the coming of her revenge.

***

Jordyn Meryl

Tomas stepped out of the black, stretch limo at the hotel. His black dress shirt and chinos make his good looks pop out. Several young girls gasped as they passed. Tomas winked at them, gave them his famous once-over and dismissed them. Turning his face to the sky, he sniffed the air like a blood hound.

She's here.

His intuition reflected he was right. If he just waited patiently, she would surface. But this time she would never escape from him again. This time he would make sure she died. He must or she would kill him in his sleep. He couldn't live with fear on him all the time.

Turning to Peter to find what was the hold up. Giving out the instructions, he nodded to Tomas as he checked every detail with the bell captain. Several men moved around and gathered the bags.

Peter came to Tomas's side. "Your suite is ready."

The two men made empowering figures as they burst into the lobby. As the elevator door closed on them, Mitch came through the side door.

***

The loud pounding on the door brought Mitch up right from a sound sleep. "What the hell?"

Fighting with the covers he finally staggered out of the bed tripping over his clothes on the floor. The knocking never stopped. Reaching the doorway of his bedroom, Mitch stopped to get his bearings.

Stumbling from the bedroom door, across the living area of his suite, he finally found the wall with the door.

Jerking it open, he glared at Snake. "What do you want?"

Snake brushed him aside as he stormed into the room. "Something is not right about your girlfriend, dude."

Mitch's aggravation level got the best of him. "What now?"

Snake paced across the room, his hands in his pockets, his shoulders bent forward. "I have been on the computer all night."

"And?"

Snake stopped and gave Mitch a look that made goose bumps come up on the back of his neck. "She doesn't exist."

Mitch let out his breath.

Of course, she exists.

"You're crazy, Snake." Mitch dropped down on the couch face first. He sat on Katrina's deck all night. The clock said noon, a no workday, and he wanted to sleep. "Go away."

Snake leaned over him and finished his insane rant. "Listen to me. It says she died a year ago."

Rolling over Mitch looked up at him. "Then she's the most real ghost I have ever seen, or touched." Or kissed. The memory of her sweet lips came back to him.

"Dude, they had a funeral." Snake was not going to let this go.

Coming up on his elbows, Mitch searched his friend's face.

What could he say to convince Snake she happened to be real?

"The internet is not always a reliable source for the truth."

Plopping down on the floor next to the couch, Snake ran his hand over his short sun streaked hair. "I don't know. There's this site tells all about her dying. So I e-mailed them and ask what the deal was."

This got Mitch's attention. "What did they say?'

"They just wanted to know where I was."

Mitch jumped up, stood over Snake. "What did you tell them?"

"Santa Monica, California."

Jordyn Meryl

Those words made a chill crawl up Mitch's back. Something about this felt wrong. If someone was looking for her, Snake just told them where to find her. She could be in real danger.

***

Now it was Mitch pounding on the door of Amber's house. The windows showed no light or life. His frustration at finding no one home made him crazy. He needed to find Katrina. He knew what Snake did grew out of concern for a friend, but he may have opened up a problem no one needed to deal with.

Snake had followed Mitch's hasty retreat from the hotel, down the beach and up the stairs at the beach house. Now he stood back while Mitch jumped down the steps and searched the beach.

"Dude, I'm sorry. I was just curious." Snake was trying to smooth things over.

Mitch wasn't buying it. "Why did you have to mess in it?" His irritation directed at Snake, came from his fear.

Where the hell is she?

Snake ran his hand through his hair. "What can I do to help?"

Mitch wished he knew. All he could think of how to find Katrina or even Amber and get word someone looking for her.

Well, she wasn't here.

He looked back at the dark house. It happened to be the only place he knew to look. *Damn where are they?*

Angry, he stomped up the beach, his feet creating large, deep prints in the sand. Heading for the hotel, no clue what to do. He could sit on her deck until she showed. Probably drive him utterly nuts. Or... He headed for the hotel's outside bar.

With Snake still on his heels, he found two stools together at the crowded bar. "Sit." He ordered Snake. "Drink and just shut up. I need to think."

Ordering a pitcher of beer and two chilled glasses, he poured one for Snake and then one for him.

"Dude, I am genuinely sor..."

Mitch raised a finger without looking at Snake. "Ah ah ah...No talking."

Snake took a large drink of his beer. Mitch sipped his, his mind swirling.

How am I going to find out who is after her? She won't tell me, but...

He looked over at Snake. His friend's dejected look as he gulped his beer remained disregarded. "How did you find all this stuff out?"

Mitch's speaking to him startled Snake. He turned to face him. "There are several sites. I just searched for her."

"Okay, we know she's not dead, but the word out is she died. Why? And who is she hiding from? She said she had been in a bad relationship. How did they say she died?"

"A boy friend stabbed her."

This news shocked Mitch. "He stabbed her?"

Swinging around to Snake, his stomach rolled from the thought she had been hurt so severely. Guess he never contemplated anything that brutal. "His name?"

"Tomas something." Snake opened up. "Yeah, then he vanishes and they can't find him. Dude, if she faked her death, and he found out, he would be one mad SOB. I honestly am sorry. No idea what a hornet's nest I fell into."

Mitch slapped Snake's back. "I know. I am just terribly afraid for her. I...am falling for her, bad."

Jordyn Meryl

Snake face broke into a smile. "The mighty Mitch is falling." Mitch's look stopped his flow of words. "Okay, we will find her and keep this harmful dude away from her. No problem."

Mitch continued turning his stool to face the beach. Leaning his elbows on the bar, Mitch's thoughts scrambled in his head. She was in serious trouble. More than what she let on.

The Space Between

Jordyn Meryl

CHAPTER FIVE

Mitch finally found Katrina at the beach house by early evening. After hours of battling his panic, he decided not to alarm her. Just relieved he found her safe, he wanted nothing more than to hold her. If anything came at her, he would take it down.

How hard would it be?
Some lousy jerk who liked to hurt women.
Ass hole.

Katrina seemed her peaceful, quiet self. No need to disturb the peace. Acting as if just being there to be with her felt better than everyone being afraid of something that probably would never happen. Snake overreacted. Mitch bought into it for a while. But seeing Katrina safe and delightful, his other feelings replacing his racing thoughts. Nothing to do with a former brutal boyfriend or Snake searching for answers to unasked questions.

His confidence stood strong.

His fear not strong enough.

***

As the sun set over the Pacific Ocean, resting together on a blanket, Mitch encompassed Katrina in his arms. She fit between his legs as they watched the sky welcome dusk with brilliant colors of orange, red and gold against the dark sapphire blue of the water.

Katrina took in the sweet scent of Mitch, of sandalwood soap and musk. Her five senses became heightened lately as her blessing with the gifts of life increased. Letting her head rest on his arm, she for the first time saw the world as it should be. Its beauty and charm were surpassed of anything man thought was beautiful in the material world.

"What are you thinking of?" Mitch's deep, sexy voice caused a desire for his touch to consume her.

"You. How knowing you made life seem priceless. It should never be taken for granted or swept over." The sweet craving to live to the fullness was no longer a cliché, but a deep yearning now.

His lips touched her neck in a pleasant, tender kiss. On her collar bone, his tongue swept and tantalized her skin. A moan escaped her lips as this desire for him, born of a good feeling, not just the hunger to satisfy a need, soared.

"Let me love you, Katrina." His voice vibrated through her body.

The magnitude from the pleasure caused her head to cloud. His hands moved down to her thighs, igniting a fire she never experienced before. His touch felt different from any other. He made her feel wanted forever not just a one-night stand.

For a moment, please let me feel this for just a moment.
She begged the powers that be.

I need to know what I gave up. It will make me stronger as I seek revenge against Tomas.

The wind brought a soft spray of ocean mist to encircle them. The cool, tiny drops of moisture heightened her ache. She turned in his arms, allowing him to move her down on the coarse blanket. Her body arched to meet his. His touch rose like a flame starting small, growing large out of control. Opening her eyes, over his shoulder, she saw the clear sky with a million stars clustered together. She knew she belonged to them.

Did they approve?

Passed caring, she knew this eternal love would still be alive a thousand years from now filled her soul with ecstasy.

Whether they made love or not.

The harsh reality made her comprehend she could not put him in danger just to satisfy her own appetite.

Awkwardly, she moved out from under him. His startled look hurt her soul, but she knew this could not be the right time. "I can't."

He released her, sat back with his leg up, his arm resting on it. His look spoke not of anger, but of accepting.

"He hurt you something awful." His honest words told her his affection ran deeper than her body or his needs.

She searched his eyes. His feelings were so apparent, she could see into his heart. "He gave me the worst pain another human being can give. He took away my life, my freedom. . ." She bowed her head took his hand in hers. ". . .my soul." Looking back up at him, she asked the all-consuming question. "Do you understand?"

His head turned towards the dark sky set on an invisible ocean. "No, I can't imagine hurting you that way." Coming back to look at her, he spoke with the kindness of an angel. "But if you need time to heal, then take it. We have plenty of time to make love." A smile tipped his mouth. "And I will use every moment to make sure you know you are treasured."

The warmth of his words made the chill of the night fade. Going into his arms, she nestled down into his body. "Thank you for this gift."

Feeling him kiss the top of her head, she closed her eyes and imagined their lives together.

Shots of images flashed through her mind. Of her and Mitch as a couple. Walking along the beach, stopping at an unknown artist booth of his drawings. Picking one for their place, he carried it as they both enjoyed a frosty, refreshing ice cream cone. With the melting cream running down his chin, she licked it off, ending with a kiss...

"Man I have this craving for ice cream." Mitch looked at her. "You?"

Katrina bit her lower lip. She forgot, for some reason, her images could resurface in his mind.

"Sure I could do ice cream. Where?"

Pulling her to her feet, he looked around. "The pier." Barely visible but it would take them in the opposite direction of the hotel. Katrina knew this was a good thing.

Her arm wrapped around his arm, her side snuggled into his body. Together they travel the distance in silence. Halfway down the wooden pier they found a small ice cream stand. Picking their flavor, they found a vacant spot on the railing.

The large structure filled with people. Skateboarders, couples, young surfers carrying their boards over their head. Katrina felt thrilled to be able to observe the hustle and bustle of life. For a year, her life had been a solitude existence. Quiet and stillness greeted her every day and put her to sleep at night. Her days were spent in mediation, cleansing her soul. But for tonight at least she could be part of the heart beat of life. With a man, who fit right in and enjoyed sharing it with her.

Looking back at him, she saw a drop of cream on his cheek. Leaning over she licked it, laying a soft kiss on his cool lips, tasting the sweet taste of strawberry.

***

Midnight came to the beach bringing a hard rain with lightning bouncing off the water. Illuminating the sky, dark clouds rolled heavily in from the west. The whitecaps on the large, powerful waves reached the height of the rock wall. The wind and thunder created sounds shaking the ground.

The Space Between

Katrina sat on the jagged rocks jutting out into the ocean. Wave after wave crashed over her, but her body remained as still as the stone she sat on as if they were one.

Her head bowed, her hands stretched out to welcome the fierce tempest. It energized her soul. Calming her inner strength, she waited for the Goddess to appear.

A bright purple light encircled Katrina's body. The warmth of it alerted her, the Goddess of Justice, Mariah, arrived.

The Goddess spoke like a tender breeze, but the power in her voice rose above the volume of the storm. "He is here."

"I know. I feel him."

An invisible force surrounding the two held the raging storm at bay. "Are you ready to do battle?"

Katrina lifted her eyes to Mariah. "I am."

Feeling the calm in the circle of the Goddess, Katrina's soul drew magnitude from the mystical figure in front of her.

Mariah knelt in front of Katrina, just hovering slightly above the rock. "You are confused."

Searching for the right words, she did not want to question the final events that brought her to be able to wreck vengeance on Tomas. The stone silence hung in the air lasting for what seemed like hours.

"Mariah. I am forever grateful for your redemption of my soul. You have given me the gifts of power and wisdom. I asked for the retribution of my life, you rewarded me. For months, you taught me well how to use the gifts of the goddesses. I agreed to follow your rules. But..."

The vision of Mariah blurred by the tears forming in Katrina's eyes. Mariah encircled the two of them with a strong purple, golden halo.

Mariah's voice rode on the curl of the wind. "...what about Mitch?"

The sob threatened to erupt from Katrina became hard to push down. Nodding her head, she waited for Mariah to answer her own question.

"He is your gift. To know what a real and honest love feels like. Just enjoy the time you have together."

The pain in Katrina's heart echoed in her voice. "But it will hurt him when I leave."

Compassionate, but strong words came from the Goddess of Justice. "Yes, but you can love with all your being until the time."

A feeling came over Katrina foreign to her. "I don't want him to hurt. How I can prevent it?"

"You can't. This is what is called unconditional love. Your gift to him."

The circle of light began to fade. Mariah floated backwards. The surface of the ocean looked like glass. Katrina stood up to bid farewell to her mentor.

"I understand and will obey. Thank you Mariah, Goddess of Justice, Queen of the Wind."

"Go in peace my child. You have done well." The purple ream of light faded, Katrina stood alone on the rocks. Sitting back down, she clutched her knees to her chest, allowed the sobs to come from deep inside of her. The salt tears would release her powers. And her mission would continue.

***

Amber watched from the beach house's window. Katrina went out to the rocks almost every night and always at midnight. For a year, Katrina was gone. Then one day she showed up at Amber's door. With little explanations, she had Amber set up her computer to set a trap for Tomas. For a month, they plotted and planned.

The Space Between

Then Mitch came on the scene. Amber noticed a change in Katrina. Whether he came with the plan, she didn't know. She just wanted to help her friend get even with the evil man who so badly hurt her.

Jordyn Meryl

CHAPTER SIX

The scene from the window was unappealing to Tomas as an alley of garbage. Young, tight, fit bodies doing what they do best when trying to appear as fodder for the opposite sex. Mid morning and Tomas impatiently waiting for some clue as to the whereabouts of Katrina. He knew she was close, he could feel her, smell her, knew her presence before he saw her. He wondered at first if she could be on the beach with these body beautiful wannabes, but she commanded better. She only needed to walk into a room, and she owned it. And he owned her, making him a man other men envied.

The rhythmic click of the computer keys told Tomas, Peter searched for the connection between Katrina, and this guy named Stanley. Patience was never a virtue of Tomas, but he tried hard to remain quiet during the process. If this person could lead him to Katrina, then he would be forced to reveal her whereabouts.

A sigh from Peter and the halting of the typing signaled a possible answer. "What luck! He is staying here in the hotel with the film crew."

Peter's word brought pleasure to Tomas. It is what he wanted to hear. The man existed, they found him. He was also accessible. Maybe it meant so was Katrina. The excitement boiled up in him almost overwhelmed him. A year he waited for the chance to prove they could not fool him. She was alive.

"What room?" Tomas waited as Peter tapped on the keys again.

Peter read from the computer screen. "Room 324. West Tower." With his quest finished, Peter turned to face Tomas. "Nothing on Katrina. However, her friend Amber has a house on the beach here."

Double excitement. The bitch on the phone the night he stabbed Katrina. Amber tried her damnest to get him to confess.

Bringing in the police and that exasperating detective.

Never would he believe it to be coincidental she and Stanley were in the same area. He could hardly contain his excitement. Finally, he would find her and make her pay for his life being made into a holy hell of hiding. But more of wanting her and not being allowed to have her.

"Nice work, Peter. Find out where Stanley will be later. Send Amber's address to my driver. I am going to pay her a visit. She will be so glad to see me."

Leaving the suite by the private exit, he greeted his driver at the side door. Settling into the back seat, he could hardly contain himself as the anticipation of being so close to his prize consumed him.

***

The long black limo pulling up in front of the beach house told Amber the plan worked. Tomas had arrived. If meeting him by herself, she would have been afraid he would hurt her. But she would not be alone. She called Detective Graves as soon as she knew Tomas landed in town. Chris hid in the bedroom, listening quietly, hoping Tomas would give her some clue with which to nail him.

Amber didn't even give him time to ring the doorbell. She wanted to appear unafraid and ready for him. If she could just throw him off guard, maybe he would slip up. He was only human after all. He would make a mistake at some point. No one lived that perfect.

Jerking the door open, she held on to the knob for support. Her voice even and strong. "Tomas. What brings you here?"

Removing his sunglasses, he eyed her with suspicion. "You sound like you were expecting me."

She held her head higher. "I'm always expecting you. Are you here to confess to stabbing Katrina?"

"Cut right to the chase, bitch. Are you willing to give up the facade she is dead?" His dark eyes were threatening. She hated this man so much. It took everything in her not to scratch out his eyes. Her body wanted to tremble with the fear she kept pushing down. Her mouth became dry, she felt the sweat clinging to the hairs on the back of her neck.

"Checkmate. So why are you here?"

He looked around and then settled his eyes on her. "I have word Katrina is in this area. Through a Stanley Greene, she has been seen here."

Snake!

His intense look put chills on her back. "Have you seen her, being her best friend and all?"

Gathering her courage, she took a deep breath. "No. Not since I saw her coffin lowered into the ground."

"And this Stanley Greene?"

"Never heard of him."

She could tell he thought she was lying. It didn't matter. She wasn't here to spare his feelings. She wanted to trap him. If she needed to lie, so be it.

"I see." She almost wanted to laugh at his contempt for her. "Well, I'm staying at the Beachcrest Hotel." Putting back on his sunglasses, he finished with the flair he was so famous for, and she despised. "The Penthouse Suite."

Jordyn Meryl

"But of course." She started to shut the door, he stopped it with his hand.

"Tell Katrina I will find her. And anyone keeping her from me will be dealt with."

"Is that a threat, Tomas?" She met his intimidating gazed.

He removed his hand from the door and reached out to touch her. "Not at all, my dear."

Amber moved back enough to let him know his touch would not be welcome. "Good bye, Tomas. I hope you rot in hell." Slamming the door, she leaned against it and took a deep cleansing breathes.

Chris Graves came out into the living area. Amber's eyes were watering, not from fear, but from pure anger. She pushed away from the door.

"He's falling for the trap. Except. . ." Amber paused and thought about not what Tomas said but how. ". . .Stanley Greene is in trouble."

"Who's Stanley Greene?"

Amber forgot the detective knew nothing about the film crew or Mitch. Chris turned to her for the answer, but Amber's mind raced ahead of her. She needed to get to Snake and Mitch.

"A guy here filming a TV series. I need to warn him. He's at the same hotel as Tomas. Oh, crap, this is not good." Leaving the detective standing with no answers, Amber turned. Flinging open the door leading to the beach, she bounded down the stairs and on to the soft sand.

Half walking, half running, her chest became tight. She stopped at one point and looked to the road above the beach. She caught the glimpse of the black limo lurching. So Tomas was staking her to see if she would lead him to Snake.

Damn!

56

She didn't think before she left the house. Her fear overshadowed her logic.

She sat down cross-leg on the ground and gazed out at the waves as they crashed against the rocks creating a fortress from the rough winds. The sky turned dark in the north, the sign of a storm coming. Hours away, but it would probably inflict havoc on the coastal town, forcing everyone to anchor down for the duration.

Right now she needed to wait and think. Maybe she could wait out Tomas. As long as he watched her, he couldn't find Snake. Stretching out she took the pose of lounging on the beach. Several neighbors came by and chatted. She talked and laughed with them, keeping her radar up.

One of her distant neighbors, a middle-aged mild-manner man named Frank, came by with his golden retriever. As the dog bound on Amber, knocking her on her back, she looked up in time to see the limo move up and out of sight.

As Frank pulled his dog off of her, she stood up, brushing the sand off. "Where you headed, Frank?" A plan came to mind.

"Just to the walkway."

Amber linked her arm through his, using his body to block the dark car's view of her. "Great, I'll walk with you."

She petted the large, friendly dog, hoping her guise fooled Tomas enough to leave so she could get to Snake.

His car lingered, then after several minutes picked up speed and headed towards the hotel. Reaching the walkway, Amber released Frank's arm. "Thanks for the escort, Frank and Bobo." She took the back way to the hotel.

Now she needed a way to find Snake to warn him. She wondered what he did to get in Tomas' sight. Whatever he did, it put him right in the crosshairs.

Jordyn Meryl

Coming up behind the filming, she remained in the foliage, watching for Snake or Tomas. She needed her mind sharp and thinking ahead of the vile and deceptive mind of Tomas. He would watch her hoping to find Snake. His attention then would then turn on him. Waiting for Katrina to show. But Tomas only waited so long. Then he would insist they tell him where she could be.

What was so ironic, Katrina had every intention of confronting Tomas. Ready for him, it took a year, but Katrina grew strong enough to do battle with him now. Amber watched her friend grow tough and sure of her purpose. The control belonged to her now.

Across the beach, a film crew followed two men on sand buggies. Mitch and Snake were chasing a 'bad guy'. Moving as if they knew how to handle a villain of murderous intent, Amber almost found it funny. A real bad guy stalked them with no script to tell them the ending.

She remained behind the brush until she heard the director call, "Cut."

Snake left the group and walked over to the table full of drinks and food, picked a bottle of water out of the tub of ice and took a large gulp. Amber wait and when he glanced her way, she motioned to him.

Ambling over to her in Snake's woman magnet style, his face lit up as if he knew she wanted him. "Hey lovely lady. Come to see the Snake Man?"

Amber circled to the back of the palm tree, leaning her back against its trunk. Snake pressed against her, his hand leaning on the tree just above her head, his eyes daring her to let him have his way. When he leaned in, she gently stopped him with both her hands.

The confused look on his face gave her the time she needed to get all she needed to say in a rush of words. "You are in serious trouble."

58

His arrogant smile mocked her. "How so? I haven't done anything yet." He leaned his head down to touch her lips.

She pushed him away. "You searched for Katrina?"

That got his attention. He pulled back. "Yeah?"

Amber held his body back. "How?"

"The internet. Why?"

Sighing she hit the tree trunk with the back of her head. "A stupid dangerous thing to do."

Snake straightened up, his mood changing to ire. "Mitch said the same thing. What's the big deal?"

"There's a man looking for her. He's here. In the same hotel as you. And he also is looking for a Stanley Greene." Folding her arm across her chest, she hoped he found the point.

"Well, okay. I'll meet with him. Tell him, I was just curious about this model. Found out she was dead. End of story." He shrugged his shoulders. "I know you want her to stay hidden, so no big deal. It's all good."

Amber searched his naive eyes. He actually didn't get it. "You don't talk to Tomas. He'll dominate you. He will never believe your lame-brain story."

"So what do you want me to do?" He stepped away and put his hands in the back pockets of his jeans.

Amber's heart softened towards him. Taking a step, she softly laid her hands on his waist. Snake wasn't a bad guy when he wasn't being cocky and intrusive. "Be careful. Try to avoid him, but if he finds you, get away from him fast. He is not someone you want to mess with."

Snake ran his fingers down Amber's cheeks. His touch warm and sensual. The huge block of fear she carried in her gut shrunk. She had warned him.

Drilling her emerald-green eyes into his, she said with a deep compassion. "Please be careful."

For a moment, they stood looking at each other. Voices sounded behind them in muted tones. A fine mist from the damp foliage brushed their face. Snake's hand moved to the back of her neck bringing her to him.

"What's going on?" Mitch's voice broke the spell.

The couple stepped back away from each other. Amber broke the silence hanging between them. She and Snake spoke at the same time.

Snake. "Some guy...."

Amber. "Tomas is..." she laid her hand on Snake's arm, he stopped speaking and let her talk. "...Tomas is here looking for Katrina."

The shock in Mitch's eyes radiated as he looked from one to another. "The guy who hurt her?"

Amber nodded, squeezed Snake's arm. "He traced her through Stanley Greene."

Mitch turned his look of fear to his friend. "Oh, man."

"Look. We find this guy and tell him we know nothing." Snake still thought of it all as simple. Mitch nodded.

"He'll leave, and she will be safe." The two jocks nodded in agreement.

Amber shook her head. "No. You need to stay away from him. Katrina has a plan."

Mitch's voice deepened an octave. "Look, we can handle some bully. Just..."

"Just stay out of it." Amber released her hold on Snake, stepped back with her hands on her hips, addressing the two men. "Katrina needs to do this. Stay away from him." Her voice sharp, then she lowered it. "Please?" Her questioning eyes darted between them.

"Fine." Mitch held up his hands. "She can handle it. I get it." Amber caught the eye's exchange with the two. They were patronizing her.

Her temper reached its end of her control. "Leave it alone. Avoid Tomas at all cost. Katrina has her ways to deal with him"

"And how do you know for sure, Amber? How do know this time he won't certainly kill her?" Mitch's true feeling for her friend came through his words. Katrina deserved his love.

Amber pushed passed the two guys. "Don't listen to me, you idiots." Stomping across the warm sand, she murmured to herself.

I warned them. I did my best.

Please don't let them get hurt.

Her fear for them made her offer it up like a prayer. Then the anger came back.

Even if they are stupid alpha males!

***

Mitch and Snake stood side by side watching Amber stomp away.

"She's downright pissed." Mitch's observation seemed obtuse.

Snake slaps him on the back. "You think?"

Mitch rubbed his shoulder. "So what are we going to do?"

"Mr. Greene." The sing-song voice of the bell hop made the two turn.

Snake raised his hand slightly. "Here."

The bell boy recognized Snake and made a bee-line for him. "Message for you."

He handed Snake a white piece of folded paper. Digging in his pocket, Snake handed the boy a ten-dollar bill in exchange for the paper. Bowing the boy left as Mitch came up to Snake's side. "Who's it from?"

"Doesn't say." Snake read the note out loud.

Meet me in the bar at 8:00 tonight.

I have exciting plans for your acting future.

The note unsigned, Mitch and Snake said together. "Tomas."

***

The storm hit the coastline as soon as Amber got back to the beach house. Detective Graves had left, and Amber was glad. She knew she would have to explain all this, but sometimes even she couldn't believe it.

Pouring a glass of wine, Amber sat next to the large windows and watched the rain beat against the panes. Her mind went back to the night her phone rang.

Katrina.

Amber pushed the answer button, but when she said hello, no one talked. Instead, she heard Tomas' threatening voice. The sound of a slap then, nothing, but she wasn't disconnected.

Putting the phone on speaker, she grabbed her car keys and ran outside, hitting the remote button. She could be at Katrina's in fifteen minutes.

Tomas was yelling, but Katrina said very little. A long pause.

Amber drove with one hand listening, trying to hear anything. Then Tomas's vile words alerted her it had turned worse. Putting one line on hold, she dialed 911. Giving Katrina's address she emphasized how crucial it was to get there immediately.

Clinking back to Katrina, she heard Tomas' last words and something go thump. One block away, she heard the phone disconnect. Screeching up to the house, she jumped out of the car, bound the stairs two at a time. The front door stood open. She remembers thinking to be on guard for Tomas, but when she saw Katrina on the kitchen floor, a pool of bright-red blood surrounding her body. She ran towards her. On her knees, she skidded to her friend's body. A large gash poured blood from her stomach.

Amber grabbed Katrina's hand. Holding it to her cheek, Amber begged. "Don't leave me! Live damn it, live!"

Footsteps sounded behind Amber, the scrunching of leather and the words, "Police." A policewoman came to Amber, kneeled down. Speaking into the mic on her shoulder, she asked for an ambulance. Looking up, Amber saw several officers roaming through the room.

As the Gurney was wheeled into the house, one young officer said. "No one else is here."

Amber crawled back away from Katrina, letting her friend's hand falls from her grip. The young EMTs worked over Katrina.

"Ma'am." A female voice spoke to her. Amber look up at the face of the first person she had seen of the police. The kind female face begged her for answers.

Amber couldn't speak. Her wide opened eyes just stared at the person. The sound of leather as the women knelt down, placing her hand on Amber's arm.

"Detective Graves. Do you know who did this?" The woman asked.

Amber nodded, looked down at the phone she still gripped in her hand. Blood dripped from her fingers, her clothes were covered with the scarlet liquid.

<u>My friend's blood.</u>

Lifting her hand, she offered the phone to the woman.
"You recorded it?"

Jordyn Meryl

Her eyes searched the woman's face. She nodded.

Tell me she's okay. Alive.

Her soul screamed, but the words never left Amber's throat.

After taking the phone from Amber, the policewoman lifted her limp body to walk with her to the squad car.

Amber couldn't concentrate on anything. The world stood still for what seemed like forever.

CHAPTER SEVEN

Mitch and Snake waited at the bar for Tomas to show. It didn't take long for the imposing figure to present itself. People in the bar parted as if Moses swept his shaft across them.

Mitch leaned against the bar, anger building for the man who hurt Katrina. Men who hit woman were despicable. Stabbing her, unthinkable.

The man moved with the ease of a cat. Mitch couldn't ignore that Tomas commanded the area in which he occupied. The women stood in admiration. The men in jealousy. Mitch in neither. He just wanted to punch his lights out.

Seeing the two men at the bar, Tomas dismissed the rest of the people in the room and went straight to them.

His eyes searched the faces. "Stanley?"

Snake straightened up. "That would be me. Snake to my friends, but you can call me Mr. Greene."

A spark of humor touched Tomas' lips. His eyes went to Mitch. "And your friend?"

Mitch didn't move. "Your worse nightmare."

A wry chuckle left Tomas. "Whatever." He turned his attention back to Snake. "Mr. Greene, I have become aware of your search for Katrina."

"Yeah. So?"

Tomas chuckled. "We seem to have a common interest."

Snake took on Tomas' stern look. "I doubt we have anything in common."

"Anyway. Have you found her?"

"No."

"Why were you searching?"

"Some of the crew talked about this beautiful model who died. Some piece of shit stabbed her. Was that you?"

Tomas didn't answer the question. "So you have no idea where she is?"

"Oh, I know where she is." Snake took a sip of his beer, winked at Mitch.

"Where?" Tomas couldn't hide his excitement.

In a droll voice, Snake let a smile crease his eyes. "A small cemetery in Michigan I believe."

Mitch never saw such fury rise so quickly. Tomas pushed his finger into Snake's chest. "Don't mess with me. I will be watching you, and as soon as she 'appears, I will take care of you and her. Do you understand?" Tomas' raised voice stopped all the talking in the bar.

Snake looked down at the finger still on his chest. Slowly, he let his gaze come up to Tomas' face. "If you believe in ghosts, sure I'll let you know as soon as she appears'."

With a huff, Tomas turned and made a grand exit from the bar.

Snake took a gulp of beer. "Damn. That is one scary dude."

"He is consumed with finding her. Like he's possessed." Mitch watched the dark figure pass the large glass windows.

"So buddy..." Snake turned around to pick up the pitcher of beer on the counter. "Finished. Good riddance to scum trash."

Thoughts crashed through Mitch's head.

This is not over. This man reeks of nasty and meanness. Bad ass walking.

"Don't underestimate him. He will be back."

Naive Snake laughed. "I think you're wrong dude. He's history."

Mitch shook his head.

No ole' buddy. I feel it in my gut.

***

"Stupid, son-of-a-bitch. Who does he think he is messing with? I'll squash him like a bug." The ire in Tomas turned his face a crimson red. Peter grew afraid he would literally explode.

Sitting still, Peter watched his boss paced like a lion from the suite outside to the balcony. Afraid to speak, Peter let Tomas throw his tantrum. He had seen them before. Sometimes they ended in violence if Tomas became confronted on his behavior. Peter learned to just stay out of his way.

Sipping the cold, fruity flavor of his tropical drink, Peter listened to the rants. This Stanley person must not have taken Tomas seriously. Repeating the name of 'Mr. Greene', Tomas wanted to kill. Not an idle threat. Peter helped Tomas after he stabbed Katrina. He got his boss on a private jet out of the country.

Do I feel guilty about it? Yes.

Did I have another choice? No.

Just a matter of time until the Katrina ordeal came to an end. Either Tomas did kill her, and will be caught, or she is alive and will catch him.

Tomas stopped in front of Peter. "Well?"

Peter had not been paying attention. "Sorry, Sir. Your question?"

"It wasn't a question. It was an order. Contact Warren."

"Yes Sir." Peter angled around so he could pass by Tomas' body blocking him. "Right away."

Jumping into his desk chair, he swung into action at the computer.

Tomas requests you presence ASAP.

***

As the people of the film crew filtered up to the bar, Warren scanned their face discreetly, but didn't see this Stanley person. Peter had given Warren a picture of the guy when Warren answered Tomas's distress signal.

Tomas demanded as soon as his requests were sent to be answered. Warren hadn't done a real job for him in the last year. A retainer would be sent to Warren's Swiss bank account every month with the instructions.

Find her.

Try as he may, he could not find a trail for Katrina. But why argue with a man with money and an obsession.

This time when he met with Peter, the instructions were to follow a man named Stanley Greene. Snake for short.

Leaving his bar stool, with a drink in his hand, he mingled in and out of the crowd. Looking like a regular guy, khaki shorts and a beer t-shirt to blend. He worked at getting the half-shaven look, so many young men wore these days. Young, good body, nice life, and with people like Tomas as clients, somewhat rich.

Still no Snake.

The hotel sported several bars, but he asked around and from his observations, this should be "his bar".

Walking to the edge of the gathering, he searched the beach. No sign of him.

Maybe he went inside.

The day was a perfect temperature, but the hotel felt cooler. If filming had been outside the better part of the day, maybe the cool inside was more for him.

The Space Between

The blast of frosty air hit him instantly, his eyes needed to adjust from coming in from the bright glare of the sun. The bar sat to his left. He sauntered around the lobby, about to enter the darkened lounge when he saw two men sitting at a back table. They couldn't see him as well as he could see them, but then they weren't looking. One of them looked like this Snake person.

Warren wanted to get close enough to hear, but not be noticed. Moving along the outskirts of the tables, he positioned himself just behind their table. Neither of the men knew him, so he saw no problem there. He leaned on the large, wooden pole and acted as if scoping out chicks. The conversation drifted over to him.

The other guy spoke laying out a plan on the table with just his fingers. "If we move over there, it will create a blind side."

Snake leaned back and almost touched Warren. "Thinking that's a good plan, but will she go for it?"

The good-looking other one shrugged. "Does she have a choice?"

"She must be made to understand." As Snake spoke his voice went lower as he moved towards the other person, Warren strained to hear.

The dude leaned in so his and Snake's face were almost touching. "She trusts me. I can make her understand."

Warren leaned in, listening so intent he almost fell over. He did, however, brush Snake's back. Hoping Snake didn't notice, he moved to the other side of the pole. Snake jerked around and scooted his chair back. "Hey scum ball."

Warren knew they made him. The other guy came around the table. His look was not one of the most welcoming. Warren backed away, bumped into another table. He straightened up.

Might as well fight and get it over with.

Jordyn Meryl

"Who the hell are you?" The other dude closed in.

Warren threw up his hands. "No one, just looking for some beach action."

Snake closed in on his other side. "Wrong, bunko. We saw you come in. And word of you wandering around was relayed to us. Who are you looking for?"

Warren never gave in. "Got the wrong info guys. I don't know either of you...wait aren't you in that show?"

Snake chuckled. "Nice try, but we've been waiting for a tough guy to show up from Tomas."

"What makes you think it's me? Who the hell is Tomas?"

"You look like a tough guy." The other guy eyed Warren with a suspicious frown.

Warren didn't know whether to be flattered or insulted. "And just what does a tough-guy look like." Turning to face the Robin to Snake's Batman. "Who the hell are you?"

"The other half of mean." The second one seemed to be a cocky shit.

What's his issue?

Snake sneered. "You look like you think you're tough. So what's your assignment? Find this ghost Tomas is chasing?"

The look of surprise Warren tried to hide betrayed him. "Okay, have you seen her?" He slid out a chair. Sat down waited for the answer.

"She does not exist. She's gone. She's dead. Dead. Tell him to get a life." Snake bent down and spoke in Warren's face.

The other guy moved from the back, pushing Snake aside. "Isn't Tomas the one suspected of killing her?"

Warren nodded. "It was the rumor."

"Is it a rumor?"

"I don't know. But knowing Tomas. It could be true. Might be why he wants to find her."

Snake ran his hand through his hair. "Tell him. She's dead. For sure."

Warren narrowed his eyes. "Tomas will never believe it until he has proof."

***

They have a name for Rain, Wind and Fire
The Rain is Tess
The Fire is Jo
And they call the Wind Mariah

Katrina waited for the Goddess, Mariah. This time three came. The spirits first appeared as colored vapor, then took on an opaque form as they floated nearer.

Mariah surrounded by the purple haze was flanked on the right by a Goddess in tranquil blues and green. The Goddess on the left ablaze in red and orange.

Kneeling on the rocks, Katrina awaited her instructions.

The purple aura engulfed Mariah, glowing as she stepped forward to speak. Her voice circled around Katrina like a tranquil summer wind. "You abided by the laws of the Goddesses. I give to you the power of Justice. Your revenge will equal the wrong done unto you. Go in peace my child. You will serve me well."

As Mariah floated back, the Goddess on the right came forward. The bold blues and greens illuminated her form. The voice like a fresh rain, known as Tess, the Goddess of a Pure Heart. "You have received your gifts with grace and poise. I give your heart the gift of Purity. You will seek your vengeance with integrity. Go in peace my child. You will serve me well."

The rain stopped and as the mist on Katrina's face dried, a warm blast of heat flicker around her like smoke. The third Goddess moved forward in a swirl of reds and oranges like flames. A sharp and piercing voice crackled through the air. Katrina bowed to Jo, the Goddess of Wisdom. "You have trained for your goal with your head. Asking for nothing more than the settling of a score. I give your soul the gift of Strength. Fight the righteous fight. Go in peace my child. You will serve me well."

The Three Goddess joined hands and formed a ring around Katrina. She could feel the power of their spirits flow into hers. The Moonstone necklace presented to her at the beginning of her teachings, came to life, shooting out sparks. Used in ancient times to enhance intuition, the stone offered protection on land and on water.

"Your spiritual journey will continue in peace to the raison d'être of the pain you carry in your soul. The Moonstone will protect you from the entities of darkness." Mariah broke the circle and took Katrina's hand. As the four levitated to join the peaceful clouds in attendance to bid her well, the night sky opened to give the stars the space to shine brightly.

The waves reached towering heights, when Garth, the God of Peace rose up out of the ocean.

"Katrina." His booming voice shook the land, ruffled the waters. "You have been blessed with the gifts of my three most eloquent Goddesses. Your mission must be of regal quality, or they would not have guided and protected you."

Katrina held her head high, her eyes locked on Garth's. "Yes. I know I am blessed. Do I have your blessing as well?"

The rolling voice sounded like a vigorous thunder. "You do. Seek your justice with a pure heart and a mighty strength. Go in peace, my child. You will serve me well."

Garth stood observing his arms crossed as each Goddess kissed Katrina's cheek and hugged her then went to stand next to the God of Peace.

As Katrina's night visitors faded away, she turned towards the beach house. Amber stood watching out the window. Katrina nodded 'yes'. Amber nodded back.

***

Warren stood before Tomas. "Look he is just a beach bum makes a lot of money doing what he does every day. He knows nothing. You are wasting your time on this Snake guy."

Tomas inclined his head. "What about the other guy always with him? Peter?"

Already punching in searches, Peter repeated what the screen told him. "Mitch. Star of the show. Snake and he have been friends since grade school." He turned to face his boss.

Tomas's face lit up. "His friend. Could Snake have been searching for Katrina for a friend?" Shaking his finger at Warren. "You know. He came off as a cocky little shit." Whirling back around to Peter. "And where…"

"…this same hotel. Suite 306." Peter smiled with satisfaction.

"Check him out, Warren." Tomas kept his back to the two men as he walked onto the balcony outside, leaning on the rail overlooking the beach.

Warren pulled out his notebook, walked over to stand behind Peter. "Tell me about this Mitch guy."

Jordyn Meryl

CHAPTER EIGHT

The knock at the door stopped Mitch's pacing. He wasn't expecting anyone. He was focused only on one mission, to find Katrina and tell her everything had been taken care of with Tomas.

Crossing over to the door, he opened it and took in a breath. "Katrina." He grabbed her arms. Bringing her into the room and his embrace, he spoke against her hair. "I was just going to come looking for you."

Katrina leaned back look into his eyes. "Why?"

"Because Snake and I took care of Tomas. We told him you were dead, and that was that." Quite proud of the way he handled the Tomas situation. Katrina should feel safe now.

Katrina patted his chest. Her sweet smile felt patronizing, he noticed. "Aren't you pleased?"

She pushed away from him, her demure aloof, distant. She held up a bottle of wine. "To celebrate." But Mitch caught the unhappiness in her tone.

Taking the bottle, he read the label. "This is extremely fine wine. Expensive." He walked into the kitchen area, sat the bottle carefully on the counter.

Katrina followed, took a seat on one of the stools. "So you know wines?"

Producing a cork screw, he worked at opening the bottle. "Yeah, I have an uncle who owns a winery in Napa valley. I grew up knowing the wine business."

Jordyn Meryl

The sudden pop of the cork startled them both. Laughing together, Mitch took two crystal wine goblets off the rack and filled them half full. Handling her one, he watched her over the top of his glass as he drank the refreshing liquid.

"So sweet lady, what brings you to me tonight? You seem to have a wall up." She looked exceptionally lovely tonight, a glow encircled her. The white dress she wore hugged her slender body flowing over her when she moved.

Her hesitation haunted him. He always felt a sadness with her, but it always laid under the surface. Her eyes were dark, fogged over with a veil of something unknown. Anger? Pain?

"I need you tonight." Her words firmly spoken. It wasn't a question.

Putting down his glass, he walked around the counter, took her hands and drew her off the stool and into his arm. Speaking against her soft, jasmine fragrance hair. "I am here for whatever you want. Forever. I am here forever."

Her body slumped against his, and she released an animal-like sigh. "Just give me tonight, Mitch."

Fingers with a sensual touch moved over his chest, followed by sweet butterfly kisses. Mitch felt a stinging sensation following each kiss and touch. When the tingling turned to a burning heat, she touched his thighs, his legs buckled, sending him to his knees. Eye level with her legs, the white, dress fell in a slow, flowing wave to the floor. Katrina kneeled down looking into his eyes, she removed his shirt over his head.

Mitch's breath came in pants, his heart beat against his chest wall. Katrina laid her hand on his heart. The beating slowed down.

His breathing stopped the moment her lips took his. He felt invisible threads already binding them. As the chilly air hit his half-naked body, a heat crashed over him creating a steam swirling and surrounding them.

As if in a dream, heat, cold, vapors and color coiled and collided to rise like a whirl wind. His body fell to the soft carpet. The only thing he could bring into focus was Katrina. Surrounded by bright radiance, she led him to a startling climax crashing like angry waves on the rocks.

His arms spread out he gripped the fibers of the rug. Trying to move, he couldn't. Katrina straddled his hips, he felt a featherlike touch soothing his skin. Darkness started to engulf him.

"Katrina. What is happing?"

Her lips were on his mouth, his eyes were closing. "Trust me, my darling. Trust me." The last thing he remembered.

***

The yielding white sand created a soft cushion for Katrina to lay Mitch. Transporting him across time and distance. She chose a deserted island to give him the gifts of her powers. Bright red hibiscus flowers waved their potent fragrance to bend with the ocean breeze.

Mitch laid lost in a magical induced sleep. Katrina knelt beside him. Her dark hair fell over her breasts.

"Mitch." At the sound of her low, calm voice, his face turned to her. His eyes were closed, a smile twitched at his lips.

Reaching out with her index finger, she traced a line from his stomach down his pleasure trail. Her touch left a path of luminous embers. The sparks circled up, a whirlwind of lights and color.

Katrina raised her arms to the star clustered sky. "Powers of life, born of beauty, saturated with love. I ask for the blessings of the passion of life for this man. The love of my soul."

As she lowered her hands, light points shot out from a stone. "I give to you, Mitch, a gift from the moon. The moonstone 'the stone of new beginnings'. I place it on your heart to feel the emotions of life. Never take for granted the gift of life for it is precious, yet fragile. Always love with a pure heart. Always love to the depths of the ocean."

The stone nested on his left breast. Glowing, Katrina nodded to it as it sparkled.

Touching him gently, she raised her arms again to the sky. "Ruler of Valor, created for battle, shielded by loyalty, grant forte to this man. The guardian of my heart."

This time in her hands laid a deep purple stone. "Mitch, I give to you the stone charoite, 'the soul stone will overcome fear'. You are blessed with the ability to walk always with pride and strength. Fear not those who would choose to oppress you. As your wish is to protect me, this rock will save you from harm."

The purple stone vibrated as she laid it on his right breast. Katrina watched it become quiet, nodding her approval.

Running her hand over his arm, she felt the warmth of his skin. Lifting her arms back to the sky, she spoke. "Believer of Justice, born of Libra, sustained by balance, let this man live long and learn much. My enrichment comes from his life."

The firestorm in the stone glowed within her fingers. "Mitch, I give to you the opal, the karmic stone. The fire reflected inside teaches you what you put out comes back to you. Always give you best, trust your instincts and follow your heart."

The opal stone scattered blue iridescent sparks the length of Mitch's body. Letting it rest on his stomach, when it touched his abs the fire shot up towards the sky. The blinding light radiated over the beach. The flowers and foliage bowed to the magnificent display of fiery illuminations.

Katrina passed her hands over Mitch to bring him to a semi conscious state. As he squirmed to ease the tightness in his body, she leaned over him and kissed him.

"All you will remember of tonight is the incredible sex with a woman you loved with all your heart. You will be strong and passionate as you bring her and yourself to the heights of ecstasy never before achieved."

Mitch smiled in his cocoon like state. Katrina snuggled into his side as he came to her.

Running her hands over his thighs, she caressed and stoked him. His manhood grew. Katrina kissed down his pleasure trail. He moaned and opened to her. Her breasts brushed his stomach as she mounted him. He pitched and moaned a contented look appeared on his still face.

The pleasure exploded into sparkles that fell to the sand. The flowers around her bowed as she took him to the heights of ecstasy.

She knew it was the last and only time she would make love to this man. He would remember. Not all at once, but little by little he would recall her in his arms, her touch on his skin. Every time he saw fireworks. Every time he heard the haunting melody playing among the trees and stars.

Reaching up to the sky, she chanted as she brought him to the ultimate climax. "Give this man the gift of knowing he was loved, and he will feel love from the one created for him."

***

"Lovely Lady." Mitch whispered as he ran his hand down Katrina's side. In his bed, she stretched next to him. "I need something to drink. You dehydrated me. I remember the strangest dream. Wow."

Jordyn Meryl

Katrina stretched and ran her fingernails down his chest. "And what was the dream?"

"We had sex on a beach. Really terrific sex. But I don't remember going to the beach." He scratched his head. "Or coming back."

Releasing him, she shoved him gently. "Hurry. I have a feeling you will need to be replenished for what I have in store for you."

When he stood up from the bed, Katrina saw a small pile of sand on the sheets. Brushing it off, she watched as he pulled on jean shorts over his tight, neatly chiseled ass.

From the other room, she heard him whistle. She chuckled. The night of pleasure and one more time with him would have to last her.

The sharp pounding on the hallway door brought her up to a sitting position. She knew who stood on the other side. The time had come.

Mitch cursed as she heard him open the door. "What the fuck..."
His words were drowned out by the booming voice of Tomas as he busted into the room.

"Where is she, you stupid little man? Do you honestly think you could hide her from me?"

Katrina slipped into the sterling white gown. Going to stand in the doorway, she watched the scene unfold. The same one burned in her mind. All the players were here.

Tomas, big, rude and mean walked through the suite as if he owned it.

Mitch, angry at the intrusion, ready to beat the shit out of Tomas.

And her.

Time for the truth.

Tomas stopped in his tracks when he saw her. A look of surprise, but not total shock, more of a smug being right face.

Mitch prepared to defend her, but she put up her hand and stopped his advance. He obeyed though his face had the look of why.

Tomas gloated. "Katrina darling, you look as beautiful as ever. With your long dark hair and perfect body. See I knew you weren't dead. Nice try honey, but it takes more than your ordinary skills to fool Tomas."

Katrina left the confines of the doorway and sauntered over to Tomas. Stopping just short of touching him, her words came clear and precise.

"You are wrong Tomas. I am dead. And you killed me."

A bright aura of blue/red light surrounded her body. Transparent as she raised her arms and without moving, pushed open the French doors leading to the balcony.

Tomas face distorted with fear. He reached out to grab her, but instead got a handful of air.

She laughed. "You are such a despicable person. It will give me immense pleasure to end your existence of life as you know it. You will now pay for the injustice you did to me. You will rot in a prison that will make hell look inviting."

Tomas finally realizing the full impact of the force dealing with him. Fear gave his face a sheet of white pallor. He tried to move but found held in place by an unseen force.

A mighty wind lashed at his body, but he froze in place and could not move or defend himself. Katrina felt pure ecstasy as she pushed him backwards without even touching him. He tried to fight her, but he possessed no power or control over the phenomena moving his body towards the open doors. His feet weren't even touching the ground as Katrina lifted him up and pushed him along.

Unable to twist or release himself from her supernatural grip, he shouted. "How is this possible? If you are dead how can you still exist a year later?"

"Anger." Spoken in a low voice full of venom. "A grief so powerful it kept me from letting go of my spirit. I made a deal."

Tomas' body slumped with the pain Katrina inflicted.

"I begged. Let me stay long enough to seek my revenge on him. Let me see the justice for what he took from me. The universe agreed. You are an evil, vile man and you must be made to pay for what you did to me."

"Are you going to kill me?"

Katrina laughed. "I wish. But no. I am here to orchestrate your capture."

"Wait." His pleading voice echoed into the morning dawn. "I can give you all you want. Just name it. Let me talk to whoever you have a deal with."

Katrina's laughter sounded deep and insulting. "She doesn't want to talk to you. She doesn't like you."

Tomas squired against his invisible hold. "No way. I will never admit to killing you."

Katrina cocked her head. "Really? You just did." A smile creased her eyes. "Pay backs are a bitch, Tomas."

The sound of Amber and Chris busting through the apartment door brought Katrina's focus around to them. Chris' eyes were large with disbelief. Amber's eyes begged her friend to let justice take over.

Katrina bowed her head and stepped back. "You can't hurt me anymore, Tomas." Katrina lowered her arms.

Tomas' mean-spirited voice spat out his venom. "No, but I can hurt your boy over there."

As her powers released Tomas, he moved towards Mitch. Mitch's face white with anger dared him to bring it on.

The Space Between

As soon as Katrina felt Tomas' intent, she swept her arm over him. The force of her spirit threw him backwards. Fighting the unknown force he lashed out against the spell holding him. Holding him back as he fought, Katrina increased her strength. In one last shove, Tomas charged for Mitch. A knife now in his hand. The glint of the steel flashed in the sun light.

With all the power in her, she screamed. "No!"

A mighty wind caught Tomas, sending him sprawling onto the balcony. As his body hit the railing with the great force, it gave way. Grabbing at air, he fell backwards. Spiraling downward his screams could be heard until there was the sound of an impact, then silence.

Katrina floated over where once the railing stood. Looking down, she saw Tomas impaled on the spike of the fence below.

Seeing his last breath escape his lips, she knew she had come full circle. The price paid. Knowing death finally came, she watched as his spirit left his body. A fiery anger blast sank into the earth, and then gone. As virtuous as she thought vengeance would feel, she felt sad for all the sorrow the first act of violence began. And the sorrow she would leave behind.

A soft female voice surrounded her soul. "Come home my child. You have served me well."

Still surrounded by the blue/red light, she asked one last request. "Let me explain to him, please?"

"You may."

Katrina turned to Mitch, who stood plastered against a wall watching in horror the scene taking place.

How she loved him. His eyes begged her to tell him this was a dream, not real.

"I'm sorry, Mitch. You weren't part of the plan. You were a gift to me, so I could go in peace to the other side."

He didn't say anything, just stared.

Jordyn Meryl

"I do love you so." Her body evaporated in a wispy mist vanishing into the morning air, leaving behind the scent of jasmine.

Mitch slid down the wall and hit the floor with a thud.

CHAPTER NINE

Amber and the detective arrived at the hotel just as a crowd started forming under the balcony, when they heard Tomas' panic screaming. No one could see why he was yelling.

"What the..."Detective Graves started, but Amber already on a dead run towards the building. She knew Mitch would be up there.

Pounding on the elevator buttons, she grew impatience and went for the stairs. His room was located on the third floor. Gasping for air as she finally tugged open the metal door at his floor, running down the hall to his suite. His door stood open. Stopping at the door frame, she looked around for him.

Chris ran right behind her. When they first saw Katrina, her form stood still transparent. She lowered her arms and nodded to Amber. Watching in horror, she stared at Tomas as he transfixed his fury from the foe he couldn't hurt to the one he could. Katrina's quick reaction sent Tomas to his death.

Tears filled Amber's eyes as she witnessed Katrina's final goodbye to Mitch. When her friend vanished into thin air, Amber heard the gasp from Chris.

Hearing the sound of something hitting the floor, Amber turned her attention to Mitch. He just sat there, his back against the wall, his face stark white. His knees drawn up to his chest, his arms wrapped around them. Approaching him quietly she, touched him lightly so not to scare him. He didn't finch, but neither did he look at her.

Jordyn Meryl

"Mitch?" She never witnessed a person in shock, but he looked as if he saw a ghost. Well, he did.

"Mitch." Her tone firmer, she moved into his line of vision. His eyes were fixed straight ahead. "Talk to me. Tell me you're okay."

He still didn't answer her.

Grabbing both his arms, she started shaking him when he finally focused on her.

His voice low and raspy. His eyes pleading to have someone make some scene of what he just saw.

"Amber. What the fuck just happened here?"

Amber helped Mitch up from the floor when Snake burst into the suite. Pushing passed the detective, he stopped short when he saw Mitch and Amber. Guiding Mitch to the couch, Amber took in the look of horror on Snake's face.

"Do you know what happened out there? Dude, Tomas is impaled on the spike fence. Deader than dead. Someone said he just flew off the balcony, your balcony. What did you do? Damn Mitch."

Mitch stared at his friend. "I didn't do anything. Katrina..." His words stopped as he looked over at Amber. "...Is what she said true?"

Amber kneeled on the carpet in front of Mitch. "Yes, I'm sorry, but she is dead."

"What?" Snake stood in front of the two of them. "What do you mean? She's dead?"

He put his hands on his hips. "Did Tomas kill her? Then you were justified in offen' him." Snake looked around the room. "Where is she?"

Mitch took Amber's hands. "Gone, she's gone isn't she?"

Clueless Snake still looked around, but his head jerked back around at Mitch's question. "Gone? How can she be gone if she's dead?"

Amber sat down crossed legged on the floor, held Mitch's hand as she looked him in the eyes. "Yes, she is gone." Her voice held the pain of knowing this day would come, and she would have to live the death of her dear friend over again.

Snake sat down on the floor next to her with a thump. "What the hell happened?"

Mitch's eyes begged for her story. Now it was time to tell. She turned to Snake. "Just listen."

He nodded.

Chris moved closer to the group as Amber put the pieces together of the massive unfinished puzzle she helped create.

"A year ago, Tomas and Katrina lived together. He became demanding, controlling and abusive. Katrina found herself in too deep before she realized she was trapped.

"Finally she got a modeling job she hoped would mean her freedom. She thought if she just played it calm, he would let her go. Then she would never return. But she underestimated his nature. As she tried to leave, he stabbed her. Left her to die. She called me on her cell phone. I recorded the whole fight. I hurried to her, but by the time I got to her, he left."

Mitch's face distorted with a rising anger. He must be seeing the vision of Katrina stabbed and dying.

Amber lowered her eyes. She couldn't stand to see his pain. It echoed her own grief. "Rushed her to the hospital, but it not in time. She died on the operating table." The memory of the god-awful pain that ripping though her, no less now. For as then, she knew it was final.

Mitch spoke in a low, raspy tone, forcing the words out. "So how did she come back?"

Amber's memory surrounded her with the night Katrina first appeared to her. "She came to me after I went home from the hospital. My heart was so broken. But all of sudden this light filled my apartment. Then she just appeared. Out of this beautiful multicolored fog."

Mitch's eyes got wide. "What did you think? Do?"

Snake sat in stunned silence. Amber looked over at him, but his face stood frozen in awe.

Amber chuckled. "I freaked. Thought I was been haunted by some demon. Scared the living shit out of me.

"But Katrina explained. Her wrath was so strong with what Tomas had done, she refused to go into the light. So the Goddess of Justice took her aside and made a deal with her. She would give Katrina the powers to reap her due on Tomas.

"She instructed me to bury her as planned. She would return to me later when the time was right to seek her revenge. So I did."

A thick wall of silence like a fog hung between them.

Mitch spoke first. "When did she come back?"

"Three months ago. She said she was being educated in the ways of the spirits. Her powers were fulfilled. It was time to deal with Tomas."

"Where had Tomas been all this time?" Mitch searched for rational answers. Amber wanted to give him all she had, but some of it...Just was.

"Tomas fled to the south of France. We tracked him down when Katrina came back."

"How did he escape prosecution? You had a recording, right?"

Amber nodded. "Only thing we needed was to get him to court for me to testify. Otherwise, we couldn't bring him back. He produced an ironclad alibi."

"And that...?"

"Peter, he said they were in the air on their private jet at the time 'someone' supposedly stabbed Katrina."

Mitch's face showed his anger again. "How did they do that?"

"They falsified the flight plans. Peter is quite the computer geek."

Mitch let go of Amber's hands, stood up, his body shaking with anger. "The son-of a-bitch."

Amber rose from the floor, stood back as he paced. She looked over at Snake. Sitting on the couch, his look consisted of one of pure disbelief.

She continued speaking. The entire story needed to come out now. Talking to Mitch's back. "The detective found him in France, but she couldn't do anything.

"So when Katrina came back, we started setting the trap to make Tomas believe she might still be alive. Hoping it would bring him to the States, which it did."

Mitch's face showed his confusion. "Why bring him back? What didn't Katrina just swoop down and kill him in France?"

Amber wanted to laugh, but the seriousness in Mitch's face stopped her. "Katrina doesn't swoop. Bringing him back became our path to justice. The spirits bound her to the place of her death. Plus she did not intend to kill him. Her goal was to trap him into confessing. He needed to come here. Katrina exactly knew what she could do. She charted the whole deal, well with the help of the Goddess."

"The detective? Did she know Katrina came back and all of this?"

Chris cleared her throat. "This is the first I saw of Katrina."

"And me?" Amber could tell it brought pain to Mitch to ask. "Why was I here?"

Jordyn Meryl

She could only tell him the truth. "You weren't planned. But she..." Amber made his eyes look at hers. "...Loves you."

The agony crossing Mitch's face broke her heart. "A lot of fucking good that does me."

As Mitch turned his back on Amber, he started to go out to the balcony, but stopped short. Amber wanted to comfort him, but she knew he needed his space right now. She knew his pain, felt his grief and the terrible loss he slowly accepted as real.

Several policemen came to the door, taking in the scene. Nodding at Chris, they entered the room. A large, sturdy male policeman gave the command. "Okay folks, I don't know what happened here, but I need all of you to go down to the police station with us and explain this."

Mitch jerked around. Detective Graves held up her hands. "I know. I don't know what to tell you to explain it, but just tell the truth as you saw it, or didn't see it."

Snake got up and went over to Mitch. "Come on dude. I have no idea what went on, but I'm here for you."

Mitch nodded, led the way out the door. Amber followed the two men. Chris Graves stopped her at the doorway. "This is going to take a lot of explaining."

Amber grinned. "I'll tell you all about it in the car."

***

In the back of the squad car, during the ride down to the station Mitch said nothing. His mind kept trying to get a handle on the fact Katrina was never alive. But he felt her. She felt warm, not cold like a dead person. They made love. She satisfied him more than any other woman.

Snake sat next to him. Two young policemen drove them without asking anything. It seemed weird. Mitch did not know what he would be required to tell.

Yeah, I had this girl. The most beautiful woman I ever saw. We made love. Not sex, love.

Except she wasn't real. Not like an actual person. Like not alive.

And I loved her.

Sadness washed over him, he trembled from the impact.

I love her and always will.

The car pulled up in front of the station. The passenger-side policeman got out and opened the back door. Mitch slid out, Snake followed. The young cop escorted them up the stairs inside the large sand-colored building. Inside they were greeted by fresh air and an orderly, tidy atmosphere. Not at all like the building on the TV set. They created it to be a place of chaos, dirty, messy.

So much for real TV.

Amber and the detective came up behind them. Chris Graves moved around in front of them, cocked her head at the uniform behind the desk.

"Come on." Her voice wasn't tough and demanding as Mitch expected. But low and almost apologetic. Amber and Mitch were shown to separate rooms. Snake was told to sit and wait.

Mitch sat in the windowless room at an empty table. There were only two chairs in the room. His and one across from him. A clean cut looking officer walked in, laid a pad of legal paper on the table with a pen.

"Detective Joe Gibbs." He held out his hand to Mitch. Raising his head, Mitch looked at the hand, then gave a weak hand shake. Drawing it back to his lap, he watched the man across from him. Brown eyes, set in a kind face, he didn't look like a tough ass.

"Mitch." His voice remained calm. "Tell me what happened in your apartment today when..." He looked down at the paper in front of him. "...Tomas broke in?"

The detective raised his eyes and waited. Mitch licked his lips. "He pounded on the door, so I let him in."

"Did you feel as if he might do you bodily harm?"

"Yeah, he was pretty much there to hurt someone."

Gibbs nodded his head in an agreement. "So did you scuffle with him?"

"No, I didn't."

"Okay, so when he tripped and fell over your balcony you were where?"

Mitch felt confusion rattle his mind. "In the suite, by the wall."

"I see..."

Mitch interrupted. "What do you see?"

The detective looked up at him. "It happened as Detective Graves said. Tomas fell over the balcony, and you were nowhere near him."

"And she didn't see anyone else?"

Gibbs stared, shook his head. "No, she didn't. So was there another person in the apartment with you?"

Mitch paused for just a minute. "No, nobody."

***

Chris and Joe stood at the doorway watching the three young people walk down the steps of the station house.

"Now that was interesting." Joe said off-handily. "Cut and dried."

Chris put her hands on her hips. What she saw and what she reported were the same stories different players. After Amber explained everything during their drive to the station, Chris knew she wanted to eliminate the part about Katrina. Luckily, Mitch still shell-shocked didn't volunteer any unnecessary facts.

"Simply case of what comes around goes around." Chris started to go back to her office, finish her paper work and get a cold beer. It had been a hell of a day. Past ten at night.

Joe stopped her with his hand on her arm. "What did happen over there, Chris?"

She shook her head. "Don't ask."

***

Amber had called a limo while Mitch was in answering questions. The long black car waited for them, the driver holding the door open. Snake on one side and Amber on the other, they half dragged Mitch to the car. Guiding him in, his body sunk into the opposite seat in the corner.

Amber turned to the driver. "Take us all to the beach house, please."

Snake waited on the back seat for her. "We're all going to your house?"

Nodding her head. "I think it would be best. Mitch is in poor shape."

As the car moved forward, Snake stretched out his long legs. "So, Katrina is a ghost?"

The simply categories Snake always seemed to put things in made her chuckle. "Pretty much."

"And Tomas really did kill her?"

The sadness of reality made Amber frown. "Right."

Running his hands through his hair, Snake sighed. "Wow. That's heavy."

The limo arrived at the beach house. The two helped Mitch into the house, down the hall to the guest room. Snake dropped

Jordyn Meryl

Mitch on the bed. Amber covered him up while Snake roamed down the hall. Finding him in the kitchen, with the fridge door open, she expected his next words.

"You have any beer?"

CHAPTER TEN

"Mitch."

He turned in his sleep. The voice washed over him like a warm ocean breeze.

"Mitch"

The familiar voice seeped into his subconscious, pulling him out of the darkness. Slowly, he opened his eyes and adjusted to the shadows of the room. Not at all familiar.

Where am I? This is not my hotel room.

As his mind cleared, it slammed him with the reality of the events forced upon him.

Katrina!

His body jerked up. Half expecting her to be standing in front of him, the room stood empty. He knew he heard her. The moon casted a bright light through the doors leading to the outside deck. In a daze, he slipped out of bed and walked over to them. If his eyes were deceiving him, then the figure he saw standing on the beach could not be Katrina.

It was.

He pushed opened the door and walked out to the railing.

Her silhouette shone as a soft crimson color. No mistaking, the dark violet eyes he noticed the first time he saw her. They beckoned him to come to her. He did as requested. Moving down the steps, when he reached her, he saw she did not exist, not in a solid human form.

He reached out to touch her, but a shadowy wall of energy stopped him. Normally, he would have freaked out, but after all that happened, nothing surprised him. He wanted to beg her to come back into existence.

Her voice strong but compassionate. "I can't."

Her words took him back. "You can read my mind?'

"I can now."

His thoughts made a heat come up his neck. "Before?"

Her laugh sounded like a song. "No, not before."

Seriousness settled over them. "Why?" His words simple, his question complex.

"And me?"

"You." Her tone echoed like that of a lover. "I did not expecting you. But the love I felt for you grew to be overwhelming. When granted the gift to love you while selfish, I took it. It happened to be my only chance to see what could have been. I am sorry."

"But I touched you. You were flesh, warm and soft. I made love to you."

The dark, shadowy colors swirled around her. Her misery mirrored her sadness. Unhappiness as she spoke echoed back from the sea. "I know. There existed only a short time for me to be human. I needed to be to trick Tomas. I used some of the time to love you. Please don't hate me. My love for you grew real. It just was not meant to be."

So miserable he wanted to grab her, hang on so she couldn't leave him. "I love you more than I want to live. Let me go with you. I do not want to be here without you."

Her eyes clouded. "If I thought it would be best for you, I would. You have a real life to live. It is full of joy, love and happiness. I will not take that from you.

"Live the long life you are being granted, dear Mitch. Love deeply and always with a pure heart. When you walk, walk strong. Your steps are your footprints of your life."

Her form faded away. He found himself alone on the beach. Going to his knees, sobs racked his body. His hurt exploded. He wanted it to end. He wanted her back. He knew neither would happen.

In the sand in front of him were three stones, shinning like stars. Picking them up, they were warm in his hands. Somehow he knew Katrina left them for him. Gripping them, he held them against his heart. Looking out over the dark, blue ocean, he saw a bright light moving away from the breakers.

The glow of the moon circled his body, held him as he cried out his grief. He begged never to feel this much sorrow again.

***

Amber and Snake stood on the deck watching Mitch, knowing he was going through some pain.

As if by habit, Amber had the footsteps at midnight echo in the house. Slipping out of bed, barefoot, she entered the living room just in time to see Mitch out on the deck. Stepping quietly, she reached the windows, watched him go down to the beach as if in a trace. With her hands on the glass, she stayed inside as he walked to the water's edge. A bright spotlight shone in front of Mitch. Amber knew he was talking to Katrina. Amber could feel her presence.

"What's he doing?" Snake pointed his bottle at the figure of Mitch.

Amber took a cold drink from her bottle. "He's talking to Katrina."

Snake stretched his neck out. "Where? I don't see her."

Amber tried not to laugh. "You can't always see what is Snake. Some things are …just are." She leaned back against his hard body. Chuckling to herself, she admitted her heart was growing fond of Snake. Baggage and all.

His arms wrapped around her. The warmth of his body brought a comfort to her soul. Leaning her head on his arm, she noticed he had a bottle of beer in each hand.

Looking up at him. "You plan on drinking double-fisted?"

With his dazzling smile, Snake looked down at her. "No. I figured Mitch might need a beer when he…" looking out at his friend "…when he gets through talking to the ghost of Katrina. At least, I would."

When Mitch went to his knees, Amber watched a bright light swim away from the beach, deep into the dark ocean. Taking Snake by his arms, she guided him down the stairs, across the cold sand to Mitch.

Mitch's head stayed bowed. He brought it up slowly, distress reflected in his eyes. Amber knelt down facing him. Snake handed him the bottle, sat cross-legged next to Amber.

"She's gone." A voice so full of anguish, Mitch searched their faces.

Amber reached out and touched his hand. "I know. I am so sorry."

"She was here." He so wanted them to believe him. "I talked to her."

Snake could not hold back his amazement. He looked around. "She's here? Where?"

Mitch and Amber smiled. Mitch put his hand on Snake's shoulder. "Was here. Now she's gone." Setting back on his legs, he lifted his bottle to his two friends. "To Katrina."

***

Katrina watched as Amber, Snake and Mitch clinked the tops of their beer bottles. Three friends sharing a secret and a heartbreaking memory.

Katrina allowed to play in her mind the memories of how she came to meet the goddesses, and the offer she accepted.

At the hospital, her life-force left her before they got her into the examination room. Looking down at her earthly body the anguish in her over whelmed her heart. Clinching her fist, her silent scream echoed through her spirit.

<u>No!</u>

A bright light beckoned her to enter the peaceful sphere. With all her strength, she fought the strong pull from the powerful beam. The light welcomed her. It promised peace, no hurt, no hate, only love to surround her. She fell to her knees, wrenching sobs rocked her body.

<u>This could not be happening</u>.

Amber stood as the doctor approached.

"I'm sorry..."

Amber's scream shuddered Katrina's soul. Her friend's pain became the only anguish she could feel. Worse than any torture Katrina could imagine. Again, it brought her agony to the surface. The police woman gripped Amber's shoulder as she escorted Amber out of the hospital.

***

Suddenly, Katrina stood on the edge of a sea cliff. The dark of the night surrounded her. The wind blew against her hard, but she barely felt it. Her spirit became her barometer to her feelings. In a black, flowing dress, she spread out her arms, shouted across the water as it crashed at the foot of the cliff.

"Where am I?"

Jordyn Meryl

A soft, strong female voice answered her. "At the end of time."

"Do I step off?"

"Do you want to?"

Katrina lost her patience for this. "How the hell would I know?"

"How the hell indeed."

The words made Katrina stop the snarky attitude "Am I going to hell?"

"Is that what you want?"

"No."

"What do you want my child?"

Her fist clinched against her side. "I want to be alive."

"And if you were, what would you do?"

"I..." Katrina felt sorrow wash over her. "...I would want to change the past."

"How?"

"I would not let Tomas kill me."

"And if it can't be changed what is your second choice?"

The fury returned. "I would seek revenge for my death."

"By killing Tomas?"

"Can I?" The hope in her spirit jumped.

"It's a choice. Not the right one."

Katrina relaxed her hands. Hugging her body, she whispered. "Can I stop him from doing this to someone else?"

"Much better choice."

"Who are you?"

"My name is Mariah. I am the Goddess of the Wind."

"Can you help me?"

A bright light floated across the water. Illuminating the night it approached, stopping next to her. As Katrina watched the beautiful form of a woman materialized.

The sparkly woman bowed. "I am Mariah, Katrina. I heard your silent screams of anguish. You were cheated of your life."

Katrina felt stunned by the beauty and magnitude of the vision in front of her. Many different colored lights swirled around, encompassing them both. Warmth entered her spirit, a promise of hope. "Can I have it back?"

"Never as you knew it. In you dwells a pure heart, a strong will for justice. Can you clear your anger and rely only on the goodness living in your soul?"

Bewildered by the question, she watched the face of Mariah. Never before did she experience such immediately bonding. The presence of this being became physically powerful. Katrina knew the physically ream no longer continued to exist. She came to the other side of life. The mystical ream of unlimited possibilities.

"I have goodness in me?"

Mariah's laughter echoed in the wind. "Yes, you have goodness. Your decency and integrity have called me to you."

"What can I do?"

Stroking the young girls face with a tender touch, Mariah explained. "Every century or, so we granted an unjustly murdered person the powers to seek revenge on their murderer. There are rules and boundaries. If you abide by them, you will see justice done."

"What are they?"

"You cannot leave the physical borders where you died."

Katrina narrowed her eyes. "Where is Tomas now?"

"In a plane headed for the South of France. He is escaping the legal and spiritual boundaries so they can't trap him. He is a shrewd man."

"How do I get him back here?"

"This is where the supernatural gifts of the Universe can help you."

"And then I kill him?"

"No."

Katrina's disappointment must have shown in her eyes.

Mariah chuckle. "Dear child. Your soul would be tortured so much if you deliberately killed another human. You will be able to trick him. He will be punished for killing you. Can you trust me on this? You will walk away feeling vindicated but will not be destroyed."

Thinking hard about her choices, she looked out over the wide void laid before her. She could feel the emptiness inside her. She clearly answered. "I will do as you ask, Mariah." Katrina stood strong and proud, ready for her directions.

"Good choice. It will take time to teach you. The fiery obsession in you will provide substantial endurance. The time will pass quickly."

"One last request. May I go see Amber? She is in so much pain."

"Yes. Only because when you return ready to fight the adversary, she will be the one human you can trust."

***

The long black grown brushed the tiled floor as Katrina walked through the arched halls of the palace. Transported across time her instructions were to meet with the Goddess Mariah. Having made a deal for payback from Tomas, she felt a peace and lightness in her steps. Two young men stood at the doorway, pulling the doors open for her. Neither made eye contact.

The Space Between

  The chamber she entered surrounded her with open windows. At the front, of the room stood Mariah with two other brightly colored female figures. One burst of colors in soft blue/green. The other a fiery red.

  "Katrina, my child. Welcome to Lockmount." Mariah's voice rushed like the wind, filled with power but a welcoming tone. "These are my goddess sisters. Tess, Queen of the Rain, Goddess of a Pure Heart."

  The form full of sparkling blue and green tones nodded to her.

  "And Jo, Queen of Fire, Goddess of Wisdom." Heat from the red sparks of the other one warmed the chill in Katrina. Jo nodded.

  Mariah stepped forward, lingering her hands over Katrina's chest. Katrina felt a chill then emptiness. In Mariah's cupped hands, a dark black mass appeared. Mariah lifted it up and spoke words to the sky.

  "Katrina's heart. Black with anger and pain. We will help her become the compassiate spirit she is." Lowering her arms, Tess held an open crystal jar the heart carefully placed within. The lid replaced, Tess carried the container to the table behind the goddesses.

  Katrina felt appalled. She sank to her knees. "I am sorry my heart is so foul." The removal of the vile organ made her feel a release of a weight and an openness to tranquility.

  Mariah placed her hand under Katrina's chin, raised her head to look in her eyes. "The serenity you feel will free you to accept the gifts of the spirit. You will know your training is complete when your heart turns a brilliant blue to show purity."

  Stepping back Mariah joined her sisters. "You will have two phrases of teachings. First the spiritual. It will unleash your soul to joyfulness, wonder and harmony. Second the physical. You will learn the master arts of defense and resistance. To vindicate with a pure

Jordyn Meryl

heart, you much cleanse your soul of negative sensations and build up your shields of positive force.

There is no measure of time. No minutes, hours or days. You will learn at your pace. For now, go meditate in the serenity of timelessness. You will be summoned when you are to go to your lesson."

Katrina wanted to ask a million questions, but needed no answers at this minute. The three goddesses fade from her sight. T she was transported to a glittering, crystal, white-sand beach with brilliant iridescent blue waves ebbing up and back. It turned dusk, the sun settled on the horizon. She lay down on the cool sand. Closed her eyes and felt safer than she had in her life.

<u>So this is death. Or the rebirth of my soul. Do it right this time, Katrina.</u>

***

The crystal stones laid arranged before her, displaying their beauty and shine. Tess explained each of their healing properties. The information soaked into Katrina's mind like a sponge. Never a struggle to remember. Once told to her, she knew it. Each possessed a purpose to unlock her abilities and gifts. Wanting to know everything and prepared to use the influence, she looked at the stones as weapons to reinforce her character strength.

Holding each jewel in her hand, she could hear it speak. Telling her of the far-off lands it came from, how over the centuries, it existed and flourished. Like meeting new friends.

The realm Katrina inhabited knew no day or night. The sun would shine while she worked and would set when she quit. Quiet time produced a need of essentially. By instinct, she knew when she needed to go to absorb the teachings and focus on the bigger picture. Night would come. No sleeping, only mediation.

A boulder of rocks that jutting out into the ocean became Katrina's place to spend her quiet time. A large extremely bright star always shown above her. She would stare at it, see her life in pictures. Her childhood, her youth, as an adult. Only the pleasant times appeared when she felt full of compassion and joyfulness.

"The Midnight Star. It comes to protect you. To light your way." Mariah's voice cut through the stillness of the dark as she sat down next to her.

Katrina kept her eyes on the star. "It's all mine?"

"For now." Mariah took one of Katrina's hands.

Turning to her guide and mentor, Katrina asked. "I hear a sound come from it."

Mariah smiled squeezed the young girl's hand. "It's the echo of its determination and promise."

"Promise?" Katrina searched Mariah's face for the answer.

"It will always guide you on your quest."

Katrina lowered her head to look at the waves receding away from the side of the rocks. "Will I be good at it?"

Mariah took Katrina's face in her hands. Locking their eyes, she smiled. "Depends on you, dear child."

"I want to be." Katrina felt the depths of her soul support her statement.

Mariah nodded. "Then you will."

The star enlarged as sparks fell from its tips, into the ocean. Floating on the water's surface, they scattered outward for miles. Katrina never had seen such beauty.

"Is everything beautiful here?"

Mariah stretched out her arms. "Yes, this is the domain of unmatched treasures, such as beauty."

Jordyn Meryl

Katrina acknowledged a kinship with this place. "Will I be able to return when I have fulfilled my pursuit?"

"This will always be your home. This is where you come back to."

Katrina's soul felt the joy of for once being in the right place.

<u>I will return. Then it will be worth the journey.</u>

She winked at her star. It winked back.

***

Music rode on the breeze that followed Katrina down the corridor of the complex.

It was a new melody with a familiar sound. It spoke to her goodness and passion. Her senses had become stronger and highly seasoned since coming to Lockmount. No idea what today would bring, her walk was brisk and light.

Entering the Chamber of the Goddesses, she was surprised to be greeted by a handsome, man of a lean, muscular physique. He wore a robe of silver, his bronze skin peeking out of the neck opening.

She stopped and pressed forward with prudence. "Hello?"

His eyes were the color of lightning, sharp, piercing. His chiseled angelic looks accessorized the air of superiority that rolled off him in waves, making him a staggering figure of a man.

His deep, smoothly accented voice rumbled like thunder. "Katrina. I am Donavan."

Katrina stopped in her tracks from the force of his voice. "You are my teacher?"

"Yes." His tone was one of indifference.

She shrugged.

<u>He's rather rude.</u>

He circled her. His breath touched her skin. "I will teach you how to fight a victorious battle."

She jerked around quickly. "You have fought the battle?"

"Yes and won. And am back." He continued to move around her.

<u>So to the point.</u>

Her hand on his arm stopped his movement. "Was it worth it?"

A cocky smile broke the seriousness of his face. "It's always worth it if done right."

Katrina dropped her hand. Donavan moved to the front of her. "I am here to teach you how to separate your feelings from your gifts."

Cocking her head to the side. "Don't they go hand in hand?"

"No. That's what humans think. That's why they don't work for them. Gifts of the spirit should never be dictated by feelings. Feelings screw them up, so they don't work."

"And you will teach me how to do this?"

An unwilling smile tugged at his lips. "Yes, I will. Trust me."

He took her hand, led her out of the chamber room. In the sunlight, the trees glistened with a faint after rain brilliance.

"Tell me what you feel?"

"At peace. Complete. Happy." She swung her arms.

"And if Tomas showed himself?"

The anger turned her sunshine world into a dark, drab bitter place. Katrina let go of his hand as if it burned her. "Stop it!"

Donavan stood back and crossed his arms over his chest. "You stop it."

"How? I haven't learned that yet."

The beautiful day returned. He took her hand again. "You will. That's why I am here."

Donavan put her through a test of emotions. At first, she was pissed. Really pissed, but his approach never changed. In a strong, silent way, he allowed her to work through all her thoughts, feelings and fears.

His tone was flat. "You have to learn to push the feelings away that usually guide your actions. You are to react only with the gifts. They control you. You don't control them."

"I don't like not being in control." She hissed through clenched teeth.

"Yes, I know. That's what got you into this mess."

His words stung. "Well excuse me. We humans live by our feelings."

"You are not human anymore."

Katrina stared at him.

<u>I'm not. Oh my god. I am truly dead.</u>

The reality rose from the pit of her stomach to her eyes, filling with tears. Donavan grabbed her. Together they sank to the cold cement floor.

"Now you get it. Let go."

Feelings crashed over Katrina, flooding her mind with images both good with bad. This time she allowed all the pain, happiness and love of her life get mixed up into one hard feeling.

When she felt her spirit clear, she untangled herself from Donavan. Her tears were dry. Calm settled around her. She saw an aura of yellow and green. The colors reflected in Donavan's eyes. He touched her mind with his, just a feathery stroke meant to comfort. This stage was completed.

***

Now Katrina wore a suit of armor. Not the clumsy, clunky kind from medieval days, but a slick, light weight metal ensemble that hugged her body. Movement was easy, she was ready to learn how to do battle.

The Space Between

In the Goddess chambers, another male waited for her. As handsome as Donavan, this one was clearly a warrior. His battle gear was the same style, with the exception he was naked to the waist. Chest tapered nicely down to a tight stomach and slim hips. An amazing specimen of masculinity, six-foot of solid muscle, a fighter who had fought hard and seen much.

His stride spoke of confidence and pose. "Katrina. I am Julian, your instructor." His words simply spoken, coming right to the point. "You will be taught how to use your gifts to protect yourself. Never to harm."

Katrina, in awe of the spectrum of battle, could only nod. She looked around, no weapons were in sight. "Do we fight with just our hands?"

Julian chucked. "You will never have to touch your aggressor. Your gifts will do your battle. You will learn how to feel their actions, their reason for their actions. They control you, you don't control them."

Katrina smiled. "Donavan said that."

Julian returned her smile. "As well he should have. Let's get started."

Standing up straight, she braced for the attack. Instead, he walked around her and placed a blindfold over her eyes. "What is that for?"

"You're not listening. Your senses will not guide you. Nor your feelings. Your gifts have their own agenda. Letting go is your first directive."

To accommodate, she allowed her body to relax. Up from her core she felt a power rise. Her arms tingled, her back arched. In her mind, she saw the gifts. Each color swirled to speak of their powers.

Purple-Wisdom to seek the right path. Trust me.

Jordyn Meryl

Blue-Balances your walk is to be strong. Trust me.

Green-Healing powers both physical and spiritual restores your soul. Trust me.

Yellow-Joy for both life and death must coincide together. Trust me.

Orange-Both my physical and spiritual strengths will protect you. Trust me.

Red-My heart force will give you the wisdom to survive. Trust me.

Pink-Love is the greatest power to exist between the two worlds. Trust me.

Julian spoke close to her ear. "Prepare for an attack. Trust your gifts."

Her head tilted to one side as she listened to the distant voices. A spine-tingling rush of power coated her entire body. The awakening inside was magical. The air around her seemed charged with mystical energy.

Red alerted her to an attack on her right side. She spun slowly on the balls of her feet banishing the assault without even touching it. Like a heavy wind, the attacker circled her body. Purple swirls moved her back. Katrina faced the invisible force. Expelling the threat, orange showed her mind that she was surrounded by five different assailants. Twisting, she simple moved her hand around and one by one they vanished. Blue swirls of color kept her balance, so she did not fear the unknown. Facing what she considerate front she clenched her fists at her side.

<u>I like this. I feel like I can ass kick the world.</u>

Her blindfold was removed, Julian's face came from around the side. "Don't get so cocky. The world is bigger than you think."

Katrina felt the heat in her face.

<u>Do dead people blush? And how...</u>

110

Standing in front of her, Julian had a wry smile. "Here all minds are connected. Especially when teaching someone."

"But I can't read your mind."

"You will. Give it time."

He turned and walked away from her. With his back to her, he finished. "You did good. With a few pointers, you will make a convincing warrior."

His praise pleased her. "Thank you."

He turned and held out his hand. "Now a few tips. Your mission is not to kill him. Just wound. Let me show you how to tone it down."

He held her mentally. Her mind took his inside hers to feel his thoughts. Together they battled each other. He was quick witted with a calm easy sense of purpose. She knew she wanted to feel as he did. Confident in her gifts, but not cocky as he had reprimanded her.

Jordyn Meryl

CHAPTER ELEVEN

The ending ceremony was attended by Mariah, Tess, Jo, and a host of other spiritual forms. Mariah removed Katrina's heart from the crystal box. It was now the color of a clear ocean. The aquamarine heart rested in Mariah's outstretched hand. Raising it above her head, she lifted her eyes. Lowering the heart slowly as it reached Katrina's chest, a bright blue/white light drew it from the Goddess's hand to place back in Katrina.

Mariah spoke with the tone of a proud parent. "You have received the gifts of the spirits, the power of the soul and the blessings of the divine. Go in peace. Your mission is ready."

Katrina bowed her head. When she rose up, twilight greeted her. She was standing on the beach in front of Amber's house. With her back to the ocean, she walked up the stairs. Before she could knock, Amber appeared at the door.

"Katrina." She started to embrace her friend, but stopped. "Can I touch you?"

Katrina hugged her. "Yes, for now, I am human. And you, my friend, are going to help me right the wrong done to me."

Amber pulled Katrina to the chairs on the deck. "Tell me how and what happened. Everything."

Katrina and Amber spent the rest of the night talking. When Katrina saw the midnight star watching over them, she knew she had traveled the right path to the right person.

***

Katrina felt the three Goddesses come up behind her. The heat from Jo and the cooling mist of Tess were now stronger surges than when she lived in spirit form. Mariah's presence stood as the most powerful. Surrounded by a peaceful force, Katrina drew on her strength.

"He hurts so much." The sadness Katrina felt overflowed into her voice. Weak from the struggle with Tomas' angry force, she felt tears on her cheeks.

Mariah's strong voice flowed over the new maiden. "He will survive. He is strong. He is a staunch man."

***

Mitch stood looking up at the beach house before he walked up the steps. He was considering a lease with an option to buy. A charming place. High ceilings. White walls, massive windows. He liked the light streaming in from large skylights. The view of the ocean surrounded all three sides.

Three weeks ago, his world crashed and burned. Many sleepless nights brought him to the decision he could not leave the beach area. He switched rooms at the hotel, insisting on an ocean view. The memories of Katrina still occupied his every minute, whether asleep or awake.

At midnight, each night, he would awake and go stand on the balcony, watching a bright light swim in and around the ocean. He willed her to come ashore, but she never did. Once in a while he would see the light pause as if looking at him, then fade into the depths of the darkness.

This house worked. The waves on the ocean created a calming, peaceful sound. He could hear it even in the house, whereas he couldn't at the hotel. Simple in design, it fits his needs.

Having no furniture as he never settled anywhere since leaving his childhood home, he hired an interior designer. His instructions to her were clear. "Keep it uncomplicated. Just the basics."

Cap took Mitch aside one day. "Heard you're buying a beach house."

"Yes." Mitch wasn't surprised Cap knew, he guessed a showdown needed to happen.

Turning Mitch to face him, Cap's face looked troubled with concern. "Look, I don't know what happen with you. I know you've changed, and I'm not saying it is bad but..." Placing his hands on Mitch's shoulder. "...Are you okay?"

With a weak smile, Mitch looked into Cap's eyes. "I will be okay. It is just something that will take some time."

Relief crossed Cap's face. "And the show?"

"As long as the location is here, I can do it." Mitch welcomed the distracted of working.

Cap patted Mitch's shoulder. "Good. We're good. No plans to change anything now. But if..."

"...We'll deal with that then." Mitch finished.

***

Snake took the steps at a faster pace to Mitch's house. "This is rad, dude. What a party pad."

Mitch followed close behind him. His first night in his new house. "Not a party pad. It's my home." The word home came out unexpectedly. Never did a desire for a home cross his mind until just this moment.

Snake turned, looked at Mitch. "What are you trying to create here? She's not coming back you know."

Usually the words would hurt, but this time, they didn't. "I know. I feel the need to live somewhere. To look at the big picture we call life."

Jordyn Meryl

As Mitch stood explaining, Snake walked around the living room, over to a book case. Empty except for three stones. One a milky white, one a rich purple and the last blue iridescent. Mitch stopped talking and watched Snake as he reached out to touch the stones. His hand stopped in midair.

Snake pivoted around to look at Mitch. "Katrina's?"

Mitch nodded. Snake lifted both hands and backed away. Mitch chuckled. "You never did quite understand what happened, did you?"

Snake walked away from the book shelves over to Mitch. "And you did?"

"It wasn't a case of understand. It became the act of accepting." Mitch never saw Snake so serious as he walked over to the large floor to ceiling windows, his hands in his back pockets.

"What about Amber?" Mitch watched the body language of his friend's back. The muscles relaxed.

"Man, I love that girl." Snake's voice sounded a wry chuckle.

Mitch never before heard such sincerity or honesty from Snake. "Snake the woman-magnet is in love?" Mitch closed the gap between them. Slinging his arm around Snake's shoulder. "Ain't it grand?"

"You know, it really is. I like being with this woman every night." He looked over at Mitch. "It is grand. But..." Snake fixed a hard gaze on his life-long friend. "...What about you?"

Mitch knew in his heart of heart, he would never love someone as he did Katrina. She told him to 'love deep'. To Snake he said. "I don't know." A half truth and half lie, but it avoided questions. "But you? This is major."

Snake grinned sheepishly. "Yeah, not what I thought would happen to the Snake man."

"Look..." Mitch squeezed Snake's shoulder. "...Let's get together for dinner. Just the three of us. I'll get some steaks, beer...What else?"

"Gee Beaver, can we make s'mores?" Snake made fun of Mitch's domestic streak. Mitch could not be offended though, he liked the sound of close friends and a quiet night.

***

Mitch stood on the deck, enjoying the golden sunset, watching Snake and Amber walking towards his house. A cold beer in his hand, he felt peace surround him.

Katrina. Where ever you are I can feel you. Hear you. Only I can't touch you.

Amber walked up the stairs first. Her arms empty, she threw them wide open and embraced Mitch. Snake came up the stairs slowly behind, jugging a tray and two bowls of food.

Mitch couldn't help but see the irony. Snake who never traveled with attachments now not only brought a girl, but also food and did it willingly. Usually it was lucky if he showed up with a six pack.

Amber stepped back as she released Mitch. Her gaze searched his face. "This is big for you. Are you alright doing this?"

"You mean the house?" Amber kept close tabs on him after the night they watched Katrina disappear. A comfort to have someone understand. There could be no way to explain what happened, why it happened, and if it might happen again. "Yes, this feels right." And he said nothing else to her.

Snake stood silently by. Amber turned and took the two bowls from him. Kissing him on the cheek, she spoke softly, but Mitch could hear her endearing words. "You're a dear."

"Kitchen?" She twisted around to Mitch.

Jordyn Meryl

Mitch motioned with his beer bottle towards the door. "Just inside." As Snake passed him with the tray, Mitch snickered. "Dear."

Snake jerked around, his eyes shooting daggers. "Don't start with me dude. Where's the damn beer?"

Mitch unashamedly laughed. "Cooler. Help yourself."

After dinner, the three sat on the beach as before, with their beer bottles and reminiscences of the night. Each facing the water, Mitch, Amber and Snake.

Amber's faint voice, still full of pain. "I miss her."

Mitch took a swallow. "I know. They say it gets easier."

"Who are they?"

"Good question. Damn if I know."

Mitch caught the action of Snake's hand gently taking Amber's. A stab of envy hit his stomach. Not against his friends for having the intimate touch. No, more he didn't have any way of having it again. The heavy sadness of the undeniable fact settled over him.

Amber accepted Snake's hand, leaned on his shoulder. "You know, Mitch, sometimes I think I see a light jetting in the water, especially at midnight.

Mitch caught his breath. So he wasn't just wishing it. Someone else who loved her saw it, also. So, maybe she would return someday. And here he would be when she did.

EPILOG

At midnight, the Goddess Katrina stood on the jagged rocks and guards the soul of Mitch. Never to return to the human form, she seeks his spirit to give him some kind of peace in still living.

Joining in with the song of the ocean, she releases the love he so richly blessed her with to swirl and fly with the night's breeze. A love crossing the lines of time and filling every sphere with its divine blessings.

It is the song of true love. Few know, even fewer recognize. It is conceived of passion and born into a world of celestial royalty. Whether blessed with it for a minute, an hour or a lifetime, it keeps a soul content and a heart pure.

As he sleeps, she lets her love for him flow to his heart. He stirs and smiles. She smiles also. He will have a long, good life. Full of delight, excitement and pain. Life cannot be full without pain. She can protect him from harm. And she will. Until the day comes and they will be rejoined.

Spreading out her arms, the stars on her sleeve glitter as they fall to the sand. Floating to his deck, she places a small crystal or sea shell on the rail.

Every morning he comes out to the deck first thing and picks up the trinket she leaves. Holding it tight in his hand, he kisses it. Her love keeps him going. Why? He does not know. He only knows he believes.

For they live in the space between fantasy and reality.

Made in the USA
Lexington, KY
05 July 2019